SHADOW CROSS

THE SHADOW ACCORDS

D.K. HOLMBERG

ASH PUBLISHING

CHAPTER 1

CARTHENNE REL, SHADOW BORN OF IH-LASH, descendant of Lashasn, stood at the railing, watching Dara as she vomited into the sea. It was the third day that she had been incapacitated in such a way—the third day out of the hundred or more they had sailed together. If seasickness were going to claim her, Carth would have expected it to do so long before now.

She placed her hand reassuringly on Dara's back, rubbing up and down, trying to comfort her in the way that Carth's mother had once comforted her when she was little. She had none of the skill with herbs that her mother had, and none of the ability to mix them into concoctions that could take away the nausea and sickness, or the pain she saw on Dara's face. She had missed the opportunity to study with her mother, and now would never have that chance.

"Is there anything I can get you?" Carth asked Dara.

Dara wiped her hand across her mouth, her eyes watering and red. Her cheeks were moist from tears that had streamed down the side of her face. "I think this will pass," Dara said. Her voice had grown weak over the last few days.

She opened her mouth as if to say something more, but another round of retching overwhelmed her and she leaned over the railing, letting the contents of her stomach fall into the sea. White froth consumed it, and it disappeared, fading, as if it had never been.

Carth didn't speak, knowing that Dara couldn't answer, and that there was nothing she could say that would help her friend feel any better.

The morning sun began to creep over the horizon. It had been a long night for all on board the ship, but mostly for Dara. Carth was thankful for the morning and the sun. It would strengthen Dara, the light connecting to her S'al magic burning within her. Even the sea seemed thankful for the sun, glistening like a thousand diamonds floating in the water.

Dara didn't get relief as the sun crept above the horizon, burning off the haze of night, and heaved into the sea once more. She glanced at the flask of water Guya had given her, and shook her head.

"I tried what Guya gave me, but it's not working. I think… I think I will try that elixir you made for me," Dara said.

Carth pulled a vial from her pocket and handed it over. She'd kept it with her, not wanting to have to go after it if Dara felt up to taking it, but didn't know if it would help ease her stomach. The first two times she'd tried it, she'd reacted more violently, throwing up the traces of bluish liquid Carth mixed for her. Why would this time be any different?

At least Dara still wanted to try. She'd probably try anything to feel better at this point.

Dara took the vial from her and pulled the stopper off before tipping it back and taking a slow drink off it. Her eyes fluttered closed and the tears that glistened on her cheeks made her appear even sicker. There was a yellow tint to her skin that Carth had not seen overnight. Even the whites of her eyes had taken on a yellowish hue.

She recognized that as a more dangerous sign. They needed to find a healer for Dara; otherwise, Carth didn't know if she would recover. With everything they had been through, her friend deserved better.

Carth waited. If Dara were to vomit as she had before, it would happen rapidly. Both times before, she had begun retching within minutes of taking the elixir.

Dara gripped the rail with white knuckles, and relief slowly started sweeping across her face as the moments passed into minutes.

"If this works, you'll be sleepy."

Dara forced a smile. She took a deep breath, letting it out shakily. "If it controls my nausea, a little sleep will do me well."

Carth helped Dara back into the belly of the ship,

leading her towards her bunk, and brushed the chestnut strands of hair from the side of her face, unable to ignore the feverish feeling to her friend's forehead.

Once they reached the shore, Carth could find a healer, or at least an herbalist who would have better supplies than the small quantity they possessed on board the *Goth Spald*. As much as Carth might want to help, there was only so much she could do given the circumstances.

The elixir began taking effect, and Dara settled into a quiet slumber. Carth watched her for a moment, noting how her stomach convulsed, even while sleeping. Would she throw up while she was resting, or would she sleep through it? Would Dara even manage to rest?

With a sigh, Carth stood. There was nothing to do but wait. As much as she wanted to help her friend, she couldn't until they came into port.

She made her way back to the top deck. At the rear of the ship near the wheel, Guya stood with his arms crossed over his muscular chest, surveying the sea. He had sailed through most of the night, staying awake while Carth remained with Dara. Lindy had helped, but she was still too green a sailor to have managed to the ship by herself.

Carth leaned on the railing next to Guya and breathed out a relieved sigh. "She's asleep."

Guya shifted the sword on his belt. She hadn't seen

him use it much, but suspected he knew how. "What was it that you gave her?"

Carth pulled the vial from her pocket and shook it. A few drops of the bluish liquid remained. "All that I could with the supplies we have on board."

Guya grunted again. "Ship isn't meant to be a hospital."

"I'm glad I was able to find what I could on board." The small satchel of herbs Carth kept with her had been all she had, and the supplies hadn't been enough to help Dara other than to suppress her nausea. "She's getting worse, Guya. I know we wanted to try to reach Marion Island, but…"

Guya's brow furrowed, and Carth noted the way he squeezed the wheel a little more forcefully. "I turned away from Marion a day ago."

"I thought you wanted to unload the casks." They'd acquired the casks at the last port city, a place called Telibuth, and Guya suspected he could sell the contents in smaller quantities.

"I did, but there's nothing we need to find there."

"Not even traders?"

"That's not what we need to find."

"What is?"

"Help. Healing. A port sooner than that," he said.

Carth watched him. They had sailed together long enough now that she thought she knew him well enough to recognize nerves from him, and something definitely had Guya uncomfortable. "You seem nervous. What is it?"

"Not nervous. Just the last time I came through here… things didn't go so well."

Carth motioned to his pocket, where she knew he kept a map. Guya grunted again and pulled the thick piece of yellowed parchment from his pocket. It had been stained with oil and soot over the years, and parts of it were smudged, but the ink remained clear, marking the borders of the northern continent as well as the barrier islands.

If they remained together, eventually they would sail beyond the boundaries of the map and would have to reach for areas not covered. Carth suspected Guya had maps for those lands as well.

She had sailed much and had faced much in the time since she'd halted the attacks in the north, forcing the Accords, most recently taking months sailing the seas around the north, traveling with others of the A'ras, using the power they possessed to ensure that no more of the blood priests remained. She had debated remaining with her father and learning from the Reshian, but there remained too much hurt for her to do that.

They had discovered only one other pod of blood priests. Sailing with the descendants of Lashasn, when Carth had arrived armed not only with those girls, but also with Invar, Alison, and Samis, the blood priests had been no match. They had easily destroyed them.

Carth felt little remorse for their loss.

There were times when she wondered how hard she'd become. How could she kill others without feeling a hint of remorse? Yet... she had seen the way the blood priests had been willing to attack. She had seen the lengths they had been willing to go to when they'd attacked the descendants of Ih, and the horror of their attack and their willingness to destroy to control their power.

There could be no compromise when it came to men like that. The only reason for her to change course was because of her friend's illness.

"Where are we?"

Guya pointed to the bottom left corner of the map. "South of here."

"We've already moved into the boundaries of the Lhear Sea?"

Guya grunted. He folded the map back up and stuffed it into his pocket. "We searched all of the northern isles for other evidence of the Reshian, Carth. We both thought it was time to start searching the south as well."

She would've expected him to have discussed that with her, but she couldn't be too angry. They sailed on her behalf, searching for the last of the blood priests before they would head south. Guya had decided for them.

"I thought you wanted to return to the south," she said instead.

"I did. I do. But for you…"

They stood together at the wheel, fatigue making both of them quiet. The sounds of the early morning broke the silence, those of the occasional cawing of a gull or the sound of the sea splashing up onto the deck, and the occasional snap of the sails as the wind shifted briefly.

The ship groaned beneath them, and Carth had become accustomed to the way it shifted with her. There was a comfort in the way it moved. An unexpected wave could often toss her, but even that provided some comfort. Guya never seemed surprised by the tossing of the waves, but then, to hear him tell of it, he had sailed since he was five. Carth had not discovered how old he was, but suspected him no more than ten years her senior. The more she knew of Guya, the more she appreciated his quiet strength, and the steadfast loyalty he had shown.

Dara moaned, the sound loud enough for both to hear even above deck.

"We have to get her help soon."

Guya squeezed the wheel with a firmer grip. His eyes remained fixed intently on the sea in front of him. "Aye."

As Carth watched him, she wondered what troubled him, and why he was so resistant to heading into port. She knew some of Guya's past, but not enough. And after all the months they'd spent near her homeland, now they were making their way towards his. What secrets had Guya hidden from her?

They didn't matter. Not while Dara lay sick and retching. Even through the groaning of the ship and the snapping of the sails and the splash of the waves over the hull, she could hear Dara vomiting. The elixir might allow her to rest, but it would not be a peaceful sleep. If nothing else, Dara needed sleep.

Neither spoke as they sat at the railing, and neither spoke as land gradually came into view. She didn't need Guya to speak to see the tension rising in his shoulders, didn't need him to say anything for her to know. She noticed the way his jaw clenched.

"Where is that?" Carth asked.

Guya took a deep breath and breathed out in a sigh. "That... that is Asador. That is... was... my home."

Carth pulled her attention from the sea and turned it to Guya. What would trouble him so much? And why would he be so concerned about returning to his home?

CHAPTER 2

Carth waited by the railing of the *Goth Spald* as it pulled into the port city of Asador. Crossing the sea had taken weeks, and now they settled into an unfamiliar city, and an unfamiliar port. Carth had never visited the south, spending all her days in the north, and more recently sailing the barrier islands. That time had given her a chance to recover from the blood priest attack, and to try and determine what she would do next.

She knew nothing of the south, other than what Guya had shared with her. He had made it clear that the south was a very different land than the north, not only because of the people there, but also because of the magic present in the lands. They were dangerous in ways the magic of the north was not, but then, so was she.

"I'm nervous, Carth," Lindy said to her. Wind pulled

at her dark locks, twisting them until they struck her cheeks. Her fair complexion fit with her heritage of Ih-lash, but might stand out in Asador.

Carth patted her arm reassuringly. "I'm nervous as well," Carth said. "But we need to be here. We need to get help for Dara."

Carth scanned the port, noting the massive ships sailing in and out. They were of all different shapes and sizes, hulls that were wide and solid in ways the fleet ships from the north never were. There were smaller ships, some with strange triangular sails that were unlike any of the square-sailed ships she was accustomed to seeing in the north. Guya suggested these would be smugglers' ships, mostly because of the speed such a hull would impart. There were larger ships—traders—with hulls designed for long journeys. And there were warships, something not found in the north.

"I thought I would come to Asador on different terms," Carth said.

Once more, she felt an urgency, though this time it was not *her* urgency. Dara needed help, and Carth was determined to see that her friend got what she needed.

"Did Guya tell you why Asador?" Lindy asked.

Carth pulled her gaze away from the strange shape of the roofs. They were so different than the buildings of the north, with peaked eaves and slate-covered tops. She wondered what the shadows would be like along the roofs. Strangely, she imagined the structure and the closeness of the buildings would allow someone to easily sneak along them. Maybe that was the intent of the construction.

The smells coming out of the city were different as well. Not unpleasant, only different. There was the familiar scent of the salt coming off the sea, mixing with the fresh fish brought in on countless ships, but there were spices she did not recognize, some sweet and fragrant and others… others almost unpleasant. A few twisted trees dotted the coastline as well, but otherwise the docks led onto a rocky beach.

"It was the closest port."

Lindy frowned. "It was?"

Carth shrugged. "According to his maps. And this way, we can find out if there's anything to the rumors we've heard."

Lindy nodded slowly. There were rumors of slavers, men who used and transported women, where others in the south favored such transactions. Carth had seen how there was more to those attacks than rumor. Dara had once been abducted to be used in such a way. It was time for Carth to do something to stop that. After what she had seen of the blood priests and how they had used women, Carth had a particular interest in ensuring nothing more happened to people like that. No one deserved to be torn from their home and brought away to be used.

That would come after she found help for Dara.

Guya settled them into the dock, leading them with expert precision. He motioned to Carth, and she grabbed the lines, securing the ship. Guya had trained Lindy, Dara and Carth to work with him, and they had become skilled in their time aboard the ship.

Lindy's face had a faraway expression as she stared into the setting sun. She pulled on her shadow connection, using it a moment before releasing it, a hint of a frown on her face.

"I'm sure Andin thinks of you, too," Carth said.

Lindy had left her brother, one of the few remaining shadow born, and traveled with her. The Reshian had gladly taken him in, but Lindy had wanted something else. Something more. With her shadow blessing and willingness to assist Carth, she was an asset, one Carth needed were she to succeed.

Lindy shook her head. "Andin understands that I can't remain with him. Ih-lash is no more. The shadow blessed have scattered. The Reshian… they have essentially been destroyed."

"They will rebuild."

"They will, but that's not for me. That way can be for Andin and the others. This is my way."

She felt much the same as Lindy. Where was home when home had been destroyed? What was there for them when nothing remained?

More than that, both women possessed a desire to make things better. Working together, they could prevent others from suffering as they had.

The sounds of Dara's retching below deck could be heard as they tied up.

"You should go," Carth suggested to Guya. "You know the city."

"The city isn't going to be excited to see me," he said. "Travel three streets north. Take a right along Oswalt Street, you'll see a shop front with a yellow painted door. That's where you want to go. They will have supplies and healers as well."

"It might be more effective for someone who knows the city to go find the healers."

Guya shook his head. "They won't help me. But you go. Tell them the symptoms and they will provide you with whatever you need to help her. I'll stay with her. And I'll keep her safe." He pulled a bottle of elixir from his pocket and shook it. "Besides, you gave me enough to last her the rest of the night."

Carth considered pressing him to come, but Guya seemed to have made up his mind.

Guya lowered the ramp leading to the docks, letting Carth and Lindy disembark. When on the docks and heading towards Asador, Lindy glanced back at the ship.

People crowded around them as they headed into the city. It had a familiar sense to it, no different than the streets of Nyaesh, especially near the docks, where it was busier as the river flowed in and traders stopped on their way out to the sea.

Clothing was less colorful than in Nyaesh. Most wore brown or black, though some had darker blue, but she saw none of the brightly colored cloth often found within Nyaesh. Men were generally clean-shaven, though she saw a few with thick beards, some shaped and pointed, and others with well-manicured mustaches. Women favored longer hair. Often it flowed beyond their shoulders down to the middle of the back, sometimes braided, often woven with flowers or beads. She saw nearly as many hair colors as she saw colors of fabric. There were shades of brown, lighter shades of black, a few blondes, and once—surprisingly—she saw a woman with flaming red hair. Even in the north, hair that color was uncommon.

They moved through the throng of people. Asador appeared different than Nyaesh, but not so different that Carth couldn't recognize the traders from the way they carted their goods from the ship, even at this late hour. She recognized those who were likely smugglers as well. They had dark eyes and moved towards the shadows. She noticed some pickpockets as well. Mostly older boys and a few girls who tried sneaking through the crowd, hands slipping into pockets or handbags carried by the women, before scurrying off to disappear into darkened sections of the city. Seeing that made her smile.

"What is it?" Lindy asked.

Carth nodded at the nearest pickpocket. It was a younger girl, one with a tangle of hair and a dirty dress. As Carth watched, the girl dipped her hand into one of the merchants' pockets and pulled away with a quick strike. She scurried away down the street.

"That was me when I was about her age."

Lindy laughed. "You were a thief?"

"We didn't view ourselves as thieves, but that was what we were. We called it collecting scraps. When you live near the docks and near the traders, you do what you must to get by."

"How did you get taken in by the A'ras?"

"That is a different story. I was brought into the A'ras because I demonstrated an ability they thought they would be able to use. It didn't matter that I was from outside the city. At the time, I didn't realize they battled the Reshian, or that the Reshian could control the shadows, much like I could. All I knew was that I had some power. I wanted to learn how to use it."

"Looks like that merchant there realized he was collected from."

Carth noted the merchant and how his hand reached into his pocket, coming away empty. His gaze swept around the street, but the girl had long been gone. Carth chuckled. "You learn to collect and run. If you don't, that's when you get caught."

Lindy could only shake her head. "Going with the shadows, I suspect you were skilled at collecting scraps."

Carth nodded. "None were as quick as me." That had been a benefit for her, but also a challenge, because she was forced to be different. She'd hated the fact that she was different than the others. It had separated them, creating an artificial barrier between them. All she had wanted at that time was to fit in. All she had wanted was to be a part of something else. That had been taken from her the moment she'd attempted to use her shadow abilities.

They continued down the street, and Carth found her gaze sweeping towards those collecting scraps. She noted several others, all with a similar dirty appearance. Her heart went out to them, and she wished there was something she could do.

They followed the direction Guya had given them as they traveled. Carth noted a few other taverns, all that seemed lively, bustling with activity, and a part of her longed to enter, but that wasn't the reason they were here. They had come for Dara, to find a way to help her. Information could come later.

Lindy tapped her on the arm and pointed.

Carth followed the direction of her gesture and saw the yellow painted door.

That was the place of healing Guya had known about.

They weaved their way through the street, avoiding the crowd as they made their way towards the healer. Carth glanced in the window before entering, noting rows of powders and jars of oils, even a few dried leaves set on shelves.

All of it reminded her of her mother. There was so much she wished she could have done differently, wishing that she had taken the time to learn from her mother. Not only learning what her mother had known of her Lashasn connection—if anything—but of the knowledge of herbs she possessed. That had been the one thing she had asked of Carth, for her to study the herbs and leaves and oils, all so that she could follow in her mother's footsteps. Carth had never really wanted to, and now she never could. She had her books, but there hadn't been time to work through them.

"Do you think this is the right place?" Lindy asked.

Carth nodded. "This is the right kind of place. Even if we can't find a healer, we'll find the supplies I need so I can help her."

As Carth opened the door and started inside, the smells of the shop assaulted her. Spices and incense burned, a mixture of aromas that was almost sickly. It seemed to cover up another smell, one that Carth couldn't quite place, but that had a familiarity to it.

She scanned the shelves, noting how similar this herbalist was to others she had visited. Were all herbalists similar in the way they arranged their shops? If her mother had once opened a shop, would it have appeared the same?

She looked along the row of shelves, noting herbs, powdered leaves, cut sections of roots, and a few berries that were dried or fresh, before making her way to the row of various oils. All of them were familiar, but she recognized very few. It had been too long since she'd spent any time with anyone able to teach her about them.

"What are you looking for?"

Carth turned and smiled at the older woman sitting at the counter. She had hazel eyes with deep wrinkles along the sides. Gnarled fingers gripped the counter. Her hair was a deep brown with streaks of gray through it, and braided so that it ran down her back. She wore a necklace with what appeared to be a vial threaded through it.

"We're looking for a healer. My friend is very sick."

The shop owner drummed her fingers on the counter. "What symptoms does she have?" When Carth didn't answer fast enough, the old woman stopped drumming her fingers on the counter and placed her palms flat down. "I can't well enough leave my shop and go with you, so you'll have to tell me her symptoms."

Carth glanced to Lindy. Was this the right place? They had come up the street as Guya had suggested, and they had made their way here as he had suggested they do, but this woman seemed less than helpful. This was not the kind of behavior she expected from a healer.

"Nausea. She has been vomiting for the last three days. Even with an elixir of delaroot, she continues to vomit while sleeping."

The woman's eyes narrowed. "Where would you have acquired such an elixir?"

Carth flushed. "I made it."

19

The woman tapped a bent finger to her chin, scratching slowly. "You're not from Asador?"

"Not from Asador. We came in on a ship from the north—"

"What ship?"

Carth frowned. What did it matter what ship they came in on?

If she shared with this woman, would she be more inclined to help them?

Guya had told them about this place, which meant that he likely knew her. If she knew that they come with him, Carth hoped she might be more inclined to help.

"We came on a ship called the *Goth Spald*. It's captained by a man named—"

"I know the ship." The woman turned and disappeared behind a curtain. She left Carth and Lindy alone in the room.

Lindy made her way towards the partition, glancing back at Carth. "That was strange, wasn't it? It seems like that was strange to me."

Carth nodded. "That was strange. I thought sharing that we came with Guya would help, but I'm not so sure."

"I don't know what Guya was into before he came to the north, do you?" Lindy asked.

That was one of the many mysteries about Guya. He had been a faithful friend, and he had proven himself competent, but he kept to himself. "No more than I know about you before you came to the ship."

Lindy chuckled. "I think we've seen that I'm not so mysterious."

Carth began looking at the various items on shelves. She noted powders that reminded her of lurthon, talisroot, and bursong, before glancing at the leaves. She noted bradsen, baria leaves, the large rolled leaves of the selia plant, even the thorned cutting from a robust weed. Those were the only ones that Carth recognized. The many others she found in the herbalist shop were unfamiliar.

She was reaching for one glass jar with a strange black powder when the woman popped back through the curtain. The woman paused, noting Carth bending towards the jar.

Carth stood abruptly, turning to face the woman. "I was just…"

"You were just about to take brethachol beans. They're crushed, and not as potent that way, but still dangerous. I thought you had some knowledge when you came here, but only a fool would put her nose into a bowl of brethachol beans."

Carth hadn't heard of brethachol beans, but she had some familiarity with different things that were dangerous when inhaled. She didn't want to risk it, so she stood and carefully set the jar back down, leaving it unopened.

"Can you help us?" Carth asked woman.

She shook her head. "You have already tried the delaroot elixir. There's nothing more that can be done."

Carth thought that a strange response, especially coming from a healer. Most healers were interested in helping, regardless of whether they thought they could offer anything. The elixir Carth had already tried was nothing more than a basic one, concocted with the various ingredients they had on board the *Goth Spald*, but not enough to do anything but alleviate the slightest edge of Dara's symptoms.

"Please," Carth said. "I need to help my friend. I don't know what she's suffering from. She's been vomiting for the last few days, and she seems to be getting weaker."

"There are many things that can cause vomiting like you describe. You say you came in on a ship." Carth nodded, and the woman's frown deepened slightly. "It's possible that this is nothing more than seasickness. I have seen that many times in Asador. Your elixir should work to take the edge off that. Some are just not cut out for the open sea."

Carth shook her head. Seasickness? They'd been sailing far too long for it to have been seasickness. The idea that it could have been, while not impossible, was incredibly unlikely.

"It's not seasickness." She glanced at Lindy before turning her attention back to the old woman. "Please. All I want is some way to help my friend. If there's something you have that might be able to help her, I'm willing to pay whatever it takes." They had gold and silver they had acquired during their travels. Some of it had been rescued from the Reshian ship, and some of it came from the coffers of the A'ras.

The old woman pursed her lips. "Well, if it's not seasickness, then it's possible she is with child. Wouldn't be the first time a woman on board a ship gets taken by a sailor and—"

Lindy laughed and Carth shot her a warning glance. "She's not with child," Carth said.

The old woman frowned. "What makes you so certain that she's not with child?"

Carth thought about Dara. Was it possible she could have met some man in one of the ports they had visited? Dara was attractive, so it wouldn't be impossible for her to have done so, but Carth didn't think it likely. It didn't fit what she knew of Dara. And on the ship, there was only Guya. He was far too kind to them, and far too accommodating to have pushed himself on Dara.

"I haven't seen anyone that sick when carrying a child before," Carth said.

The old lady shrugged. "Sometimes the first few months can be the worst. I have seen it many times myself. Know that it will get better in time. Just provide small meals and let her rest as much as possible."

Carth shook her head again. She really did not think Dara was pregnant, but it was becoming increasingly obvious that the old woman was not going to help them.

"Then at least sell me some"—Carth tried thinking of a collection of various leaves and berries that might help, not coming up with anything as easily as she had hoped—"ashen leaves, doxan berries, helfer, and thistle leaves."

The old woman's brow furrowed again and she shrugged. She tottered around the shop, pointing to various jars, but not offering to help.

Carth grabbed each of the jars when the old woman didn't help spoon out various amounts of the items she had asked for. When she set them on the counter in front of the woman, she shook her head.

"Most do not purchase this much."

Carth pulled out for gold coins. It would be more than enough for what they purchased. She slammed them onto the counter. "Since you have been so little help, I will purchase all of these. This should be enough to cover the cost of you buying the replacement."

She waited for the woman to argue, and Carth would've been willing to make a different deal, and would have taken even some of the various herbs she had grabbed, but what was the point in doing that when this woman was so clearly not willing to help?

The woman seemed to consider for a moment before waving her hand and sending Carth and Lindy out the door. Carth clutched the items they had purchased to her chest, as if they were precious cargo.

These could help, but she knew they would do nothing more than ease Dara's symptoms.

Dara needed more than what Carth was able to provide. That, as much as anything, upset her.

Once outside in the cool evening air, Lindy glanced back at the shop, a surprised expression on her face. "That's not what I was expecting from a healer."

"No. That's not what I expected either."

"It seems that when you mentioned Guya…"

Carth hadn't made the connection, but now that Lindy said it, she realized that it was true. The old woman had seemed more agitated after she'd mentioned Guya. Why would that be? Why would the old woman be bothered by Guya, someone who had been nothing but kind and considerate with them?

Was that why Guya had not wanted to enter the city? If he avoided her, why tell them to come to this healer?

"Let's take these back to Dara see if we can at least help her symptoms a little more."

Carth began sorting the bundle into the pockets of her long black cloak. She stored them in separate pockets so the glass jars wouldn't bang together.

"Do you think what you've purchased will work?"

Carth could only shake her head. She didn't know, just as she didn't know what was happening to Dara. And that bothered her.

CHAPTER 3

By the time Carth returned to the *Goth Spald* with Lindy, she was frustrated. She held carefully to the vials she'd bought from the healer. There might be something Carth could mix with them, but her other hope was that she could find something in one of her mother's books that would provide answers. If only she could read it and understand. Working through the Lashasn language had proven difficult for her so far.

They found the ramp leading to the ship missing.

Carth glanced to Lindy, a shared question in their eyes. Guya rarely pulled the ramp up when they were off in port. He knew they could come back at any time and needed to have a way on board. Though Carth could use the shadows to jump, the ramp left fewer questions. None of them wanted questions about how Carth could jump on board the ship, or how she could move in ways that others could not.

"Maybe he went into town?" Lindy said.

Carth frowned.

The top deck of the ship was empty, with no sign of Guya or Dara. Carth hadn't expected to see Dara, especially with how sick she'd been when they'd left, but Guya rarely left the topside while in port. He feared what other sailors might do. Piracy didn't only happen on the sea.

Had something happened to Dara?

That was the only reason Guya would have left the ship.

Not the only reason, she had to admit.

There had been Guya's reluctance to return to Asador. It was his home, but he'd resisted coming back, willingly spending whatever time Carth had wanted to travel around the north to search for the remaining blood priests. And then there had been the way the healer had disappeared the moment Carth had mentioned the ship she'd come on. Had she sent word to someone that Guya had upset?

"This isn't right," she said, though it was mostly to herself.

Lindy nodded, her mouth pinched into a tight frown. "Have you noticed anything?"

Carth tipped her head to the side. "Nothing. Do you detect anything?"

Lindy closed her eyes and pulled on the shadows, fading into them. What Lindy did was different than the way Carth used the shadows. Whereas Carth used them more like cloaking herself, something that Jhon had taught her, Lindy used them in a way that lessened her but didn't shroud her completely. Carth didn't know if that had to do with the fact that she was shadow born and could see through them, but had decided that it must actually *be* different.

When Lindy opened her eyes, she shook her head. "They're gone."

"How do you do that?" The shadows were powerful, but they shouldn't be able to give her that kind of insight. With the S'al, Carth could detect differences in heat... *could* that be how Lindy had known? It intrigued her that she continued to learn about the shadows, and she appreciated having Lindy with her to help her discover the different connections.

"It's nothing more than an understanding of the power within the shadows," Lindy said.

Carth focused on the shadows and sank into them. There was a time when she had called it cloaking, but this was somewhat different than what she had done when she had cloaked herself. This was almost as if she faded into the shadows themselves. Others who were more skilled could truly fade into them and disappear completely as they did. They didn't even need the same shadow-born ability Carth possessed.

The shadows let her know there was a difference here, a variation among the shadows, but no sign of Guya or Dara.

Lindy laughed softly. "If you ever come to fully

understand the shadows, you are going to be very powerful."

"I have you to teach me."

"I can't do what you do."

"You know enough. The rest I can figure out over time."

"You could have gone with the Reshian," Lindy started. Carth arched a brow at her. "Fine. Ignore the fact that your father was willing to work with you."

"I wasn't willing to pay the price that would have required."

"There's always a price to pay for power. Haven't you taught me that?"

"I've taught you many things."

"And this you taught yourself. From the look on your face, I can tell you succeeded without anyone showing you how. It took me two years to learn how to do that, and I still can only do it in confined spaces. You… you managed to simply discover it."

"It's similar to what I can do with the S'al."

"They shouldn't be similar enough for you to use the same skills."

Carth chuckled. Lindy had been around her long enough to know that she shouldn't make statements like that, but her time in Isahl and within Ih-lash had been enough to keep the old ways of thinking ingrained in her head. "They're not as dissimilar as most think."

"Not as different? They are entirely different."

"Can you use the power of the S'al?"

Lindy frowned. "You know I cannot."

"Just know that they're similar." She pulsed through the power of the flame and used that to reach for differences in temperature below deck, but found nothing. She hadn't expected to, especially once she'd realized there was nothing with the shadows, but she wanted to check anyway.

"Let's see if they left any sign of where they went," Carth said.

Lindy's brow was furrowed in a frown, but she nodded.

When they went below deck, they searched for Guya and Dara, but the rooms were empty. Dara's bunk had the sheets thrown back. Guya's door was locked. The other rooms were empty as well. There was no sign of anyone here.

Carth couldn't shake an unsettled sense she had within her. It wasn't that the rooms were empty, but that Carth had no way of knowing where they would have gone.

"Look here," Lindy said, pointing to the floor outside of Dara's room.

Carth studied the floor and noted a slight streak of blood mixed with vomit.

"He went to get help," Carth said.

Lindy nodded. "I think he must have. But why would he have brought her with him? Why not go for help and bring them to her? She wouldn't have been well enough to come with him, at least not very far."

"Unless she got too sick to stay behind," Carth said.

But Carth and Lindy would have seen them, wouldn't they? Wouldn't he have brought Dara to the same healer they'd just visited?

They wouldn't know the streets as well as Guya. He'd spent significant amounts of time in Asador and would have known where to go.

"I should have known," Carth said.

Lindy frowned. "How were you supposed to know? She said she wasn't that bad."

"I know, but I should have known. She wasn't acting herself, especially the last few days."

"She thought it was seasickness."

"She only said that to have an answer. Dara knew it wasn't seasickness." That would have made sense had they only recently left, but Dara had been sailing with her for a while now, long enough that she should have gotten accustomed to the sea.

Carth looked from the pile of vomit and wondered if this was something that had happened recently. They been gone most of the evening, but Dara could've deteriorated fairly rapidly. Carth leaned down, getting close to the vomit, ignoring Lindy's protestations and the slight sound of her gagging.

Carth didn't have the same weak stomach and didn't mind getting too close to the foul-smelling liquid, especially if it meant that she could determine what had happened to her friend. She owed that much to Dara.

The blood was dry. The vomit itself was hardened, and though there was an odor to it, it wasn't quite as bad as it would have been when fresh.

Carth frowned. Where would they have gone?

She stopped in front of Guya's door, testing the lock and then surging a hint of shadows through it, forcing the lock open. She hated violating Guya's trust this way and had never done so during their time sailing together, preferring to allow him his privacy, but she needed to know what had happened here.

Unlike Dara's bed, where the sheets had been pulled back, leaving the bed unmade, Guya's bunk was neatly made. She scanned his room and noted the lantern next to the bed, the stack of books in the corner, and the trunk at the foot of the bed.

The trunk was cracked open.

Carth wondered about that. Why would Guya have left the trunk open?

She flipped the lid up and found it empty. It had a slight bitter odor to it, one that reminded her of some of the medicines she now carried with her.

Carth turned to Lindy, who stood in the doorway, watching her. "I don't like this."

"I don't either. I know you're worried about Dara, but we'll find out what happened when they return."

Carth nodded, but didn't feel comfortable with that

answer. Something inside her, instinct or a hunch, told her that there was more going on than she realized.

She closed her eyes so that she could almost see pieces of the game board being moved around her, and asked the question she always asked when trying to understand something: What was she missing?

There had to be something, but what was it?

Carth made her way back up to the deck and stood staring out at the sea. There was something peaceful about the sea, and she often thought she could find answers more easily while staring at the water. Answers didn't come to her today.

She turned her attention back to the ship and noted a trail of blood she hadn't seen before. There were scorch marks she'd overlooked as well.

Had Dara used her ability?

Carth followed the blood, wondering whose it was, when a soft moaning caught her attention.

It came from the dock.

Carth jumped, reaching the dock, and found Dara lying sprawled near its edge. One bad roll and she would have splashed into the water.

"Dara?" Carth said.

Her friend said nothing. A sheen of sweat coated Dara's forehead, and even in the moonlight, it was obvious how yellow her skin had become.

Carth knew what that meant: Dara needed help, or she would die.

CHAPTER 4

CARTH CARRIED DARA, HURRYING ALONG THE STREET. Dara lolled against her, her head rolling as if the muscles in her neck had failed her. Lindy had offered to help carry her, but Carth had declined, preferring Lindy to take a forward position to keep an eye on them. She could mask them with the shadows, just enough that it would obscure them from others' eyes.

In the shadows, she couldn't see how washed out Dara looked and didn't see any signs of the yellow in her skin, but she noted the sickly odor, a mixture of vomit and whatever illness it was that consumed Dara.

How much time did they have before Dara could not be helped? The woman had barely eaten for the last few days, and she grew increasingly weak. If they didn't get her help—real help—and soon, Carth didn't like the odds of Dara's recovery.

"Where should we go?" Lindy asked.

Carth considered bringing Dara back to the healer Guya had recommended. The timing of their visit with Guya's disappearance made her uncomfortable. They would have to find another healer, one who wouldn't have the same bias, but perhaps one without the same level of skill as the one Guya had recommended.

No option was good.

Dara moaned softly, and Carth cupped her friend against her, wishing there were some way she could do more than comfort Dara. She couldn't take the risk that she would find a healer of enough skill to help her friend. That left her with no other option than to bring Dara back to the other healer—even if she was responsible for what had happened to Guya.

They made their way through the streets, passing people out for the evening, some already intoxicated, others likely on their way to the taverns. Some appeared to be part of the city's underworld, their dress dark and their furtive glances making it clear they looked for signs of those who might report them. Carth had grown accustomed to seeing men like that when she'd lived on the docks.

Dozens of children were found around the streets as well. Many wandered without parents, all of different ages, making Carth wonder whether they were orphans or whether they were involved in some nefarious activity, much as Carth had once been.

When they reached the yellow door of the healer's shop, they found it locked.

A lantern burned behind the glass window, and Carth saw flickers of shadow moving there as well. She frowned, knowing that it was too late for the healer's shop to be open, but something had to be done for Dara. She debated whether to knock or simply barge in, but decided that attempting a politer approach would likely give her the best chance of getting the help she needed.

Carth nodded at the door, and Lindy knocked.

They stood waiting for a moment until the door slowly opened.

An eye poked out, though not one belonging to the healer they had met before. A youthful face with smooth features over her deeply tanned skin, with eyes that were almost as black as the night, widened slightly when they noticed Carth carrying Dara.

She pulled the door open quickly and motioned them in.

Carth hesitated. This wasn't the same woman they had seen before, but maybe she trained under the other, and maybe she would be more accommodating. She was young, about the same age as Carth, and had a determined set to her jaw as she studied them.

Inside the herbalist shop, the lantern cast a soft glow. It was not enough to disperse the shadows completely, but enough for Carth to note the rows of jars on the shelves and the glittering of oil within clear basins as well. The woman pointed to the back corner of the shop, and Carth carried Dara obediently. She found a small cot there and set Dara upon it.

"What happened to her?" the woman asked.

Carth glanced to Lindy, not certain whether this woman was to be trusted, but for Dara's sake, she needed to be as forthright as possible.

"Vomiting. Several days of vomiting. She hasn't been able to keep anything down." She decided to leave out the part about her trying the elixir, especially since the other woman had questioned her more pointedly after hearing that.

The woman nodded. "Her skin has a slight jaundice to it." She lifted Dara's lids and looked at her eyes before nodding to herself. She leaned in and smelled her breath and then raised each arm before lowering them once more.

The woman hurried to the back of the shop, quickly gathering some supplies. She placed several different powders in a small bowl and began mixing, tapping her finger on the side of the bowl as she did. After a while, she went back to the shelves and found a vial of oil that she added to the mixture.

"What kind of oil is that?" Carth asked, unable to help herself.

"This is dalin oil," the woman said. "I need something to bind these agents together; otherwise, they remain powdered. I don't want to dilute them too much or they lose potency, so the dalin oil should do the trick."

Carth breathed out a sigh of relief. This woman seemed to know what she was talking about. It reassured her, but didn't completely take away the edge of worry that nagged at her, or the concern she felt wondering why the old woman had been so unwilling to work with them. It didn't take away the troubled sensation that gnawed at her stomach when she wondered about what had happened to Guya or why Dara had attempted to crawl off the ship. Guya wouldn't have simply left her, not knowing how sick she was, which meant there was another answer.

The healer continued mixing her concoction. When she finished, she tipped it to Dara's lips, forcing her to drink. It was an awful shade of orange, one that almost glowed, and Carth imagined it tasted horrible, especially with the smell it had once mixed. It was a sharp scent, one touched with a hint of soot and smoke and mixed with something she would describe as a rot—likely the dalin oil—and wished there might've been something else that would help Dara so that she didn't need it.

The healer nodded to herself. "That's done. Now all we have to do is wait."

"How long?" Carth asked.

The other woman shook her head. "It is unpredictable. There are many things that can cause jaundice such as your friend experienced. It could be something as simple as what she ate, an illness, or something that she might have been exposed to. What I gave her will help allay the symptoms and give her time to recover if she can. She needs time. If it was food, time will allow her to recover. If an exposure, it will wash out of her system. If an illness... there might be little that can be done."

Carth stared at Dara, hoping that time was all that was needed for her to recover. "How much do we owe you?" she asked.

The woman shook her head again. "I don't know how long she'll take to recover. I think she should remain here until she awakens. I can continue working with her and provide whatever medicine she needs."

Carth glanced to Lindy. Neither of them preferred leaving Dara here—especially considering the way the first healer had treated them—but what choice did they have? It would give them time to look for Guya, and they wouldn't have to worry about Dara being cared for.

Carth sighed and pulled a gold coin from her pocket, setting it on the counter. "See that she is well cared for. I'll check back in the morning."

"Of course. Before you go, tell me her name in case she awakens."

"Dara. Her name is Dara."

"And you?" the woman asked.

"I am Carthenne Rel."

The woman stuck her hand out and waited until Carth shook it. "I'm Abigail. I'm only an apprentice, but I've seen things like this before, and I'll make sure my mistress gives her all the attention she needs when she returns."

Carth hoped that when the mistress returned, she wouldn't be angry about the fact that Carth had brought Dara to her for healing. Most healers wouldn't object when faced with someone as sick as Dara, but if there was something between her and Guya, some reason the healer refused to help him, she didn't want to chance it.

If that was the case, though, why would Guya have sent her to this healer?

The pieces on the game board didn't make sense. Carth had to arrange them and see if she could puzzle out the answers. For now, she needed to make the next move and find Guya. Then she could make the one after that. And then another.

"See that she gets all the help she needs. We can pay whatever it takes."

Abigail waved her hand. "The cost is not an issue. Come back in the morning, and we'll see how she's doing. If she's doing well enough at that time, she can return with you. Otherwise, she may need to stay here until she recovers completely."

Carth crouched next to Dara and leaned towards her friend, whispering in her ear. "We'll return, Dara. Get well."

She touched her on the forehead and then stood, motioning for Lindy to follow her out of the shop.

Back out on the street, they stood in front of the

healer's shop until Abigail locked the door behind them. There was a finality to the sound, one that made Carth worry that she wouldn't see Dara again. She hoped that leaving her with the healer had been the right decision.

"What now?" Lindy asked, covering her mouth as she yawned.

Carth was tired too, but she didn't let herself feel the effects of the fatigue. They needed to find Guya now. His absence left her unsettled, and given the way they had been greeted by the healer, Carth hoped there was nothing nefarious about his disappearance.

"We need to find answers."

"How do you propose we do that?"

Carth turned to her with a smile. There was only one answer when coming off a ship and into a port. "If you want answers, we need to go where tongues are loose."

Lindy shook her head. "You're predictable, Carth. What is it with you and taverns?"

CHAPTER 5

Taverns held a special place in Carth's heart. They were a place she had been welcomed, one where she had gained the confidence to live independently, but in a way, it was the last place of innocence for her. After leaving the Wounded Lyre, she had gone to train with the A'ras. That was the end of any innocence she had ever possessed.

Maybe it was more than that. Maybe it was the fact that she truly could find information within taverns. Men and women were often quick to share and gossip in the tavern. Part of the reason she'd desired to come to the southern continent had been her hope of finding a way to more easily obtain information about the Hjan, to ensure that they wouldn't be able to attack without some warning, and doing that involved setting up a network. Ras had demonstrated how such a thing was possible, but over time, she intended to do much more than what he had accomplished.

As they returned toward the docks, Carth counted nearly a dozen different taverns. The darkness of night had settled, giving long shadows that stretched across the street, shadows that Carth welcomed. From here, there were the muted sounds of waves crashing along the shore, and the sounds of music coming from the taverns, a restless sort of revelry.

One tavern seemed especially lively. Carth nodded to it, motioning for Lindy to follow as they entered. The tavern was much more compact than many of the taverns they had visited, but like the others, it was quite crowded, people of many different styles of dress all crammed together, talking loudly. A lutist played near the back of the room, and several people attempted to dance near the musician, but there was not enough space. A few serving women hurried through the tavern, squeezing between the crowd, carrying mugs of ale and trays laden with food. Other than the crowd, it all looked familiar to Carth.

Despite what they'd been through, a slight smile spread across her face. It shouldn't surprise her that taverns were all the same. This had more of the fishing crowd, men who smelled of the sea and had grime coating their hands. Shirts were stained with sweat and oils and, in many cases, blood. Few of the men were armed, a difference compared to the other taverns.

Lindy nudged her as a server approached carrying a mug of ale.

"Five coppers," the server said. Her eyes scanned the crowd, almost as if looking for others who might have empty hands and a look of thirst.

Carth blinked. "Five coppers? Isn't that price a little high?"

"If you think five coppers is too pricey, why don't you go on down the street to the Frosted Pint or the Dragons Eye? They might have a little better quality ale, but is that worth the ten coppers they charge?"

Lindy shrugged, and Carth took money from her pocket and slipped it into the woman's hand. It was more than they wanted to spend, but she needed answers, and this seemed like as good a place to get them as any.

The woman glanced down and noted the silver piece before cupping her hand around the coins.

"Consider that payment for this round and the next," Carth said.

The woman's eyes widened slightly as she nodded. "Make sure to ask for Julie when you need another round," the woman said.

When Julie left them, Carth and Lindy surveyed the tavern. They hadn't had much luck so far this evening finding out anything they needed. Carth wanted gossip. Oftentimes that was easy in a tavern, especially if you kept your head down and listened, but so far, they'd heard nothing.

There had been some local city gossip, mostly about orphans—which Carth discovered was a bigger problem than she had realized at first. From the rumors she heard, it seemed like there were hordes of orphans running the streets. They had taken to thieving, doing so openly and angering the city elders.

Carth hadn't determined how the city governance was structured, other than the fact that several elders led the city. She'd visited places where the structure was similar, and those elders had been elected, but she hadn't been able to determine whether that was the case in Asador.

"Why here?" Lindy asked.

Carth took a sip of her ale. It was watery, had too much of a barley taste to it for her liking, but had just the right amount of fizz. "I don't know what we'll find, but we need to figure out what happened to Guya. I don't think he would've just disappeared." Not and leave Dara on the ship. And, if nothing else, he wouldn't leave his ship alone.

"The healer—"

"Yes. That bothers me as well." She'd disappeared when they had mentioned the *Goth Spald.* Could the healer be responsible for what happened to Guya? That seemed unlikely, but equally unlikely was how the healer had reacted to their presence.

As Carth sipped her ale, she held on to her connection to the shadows, using them to disappear slightly, enough that they wouldn't draw attention. Lindy did the same. They masked themselves, nothing more than that.

Carth weaved around the tavern as she remained shrouded in the shadows, listening as she went. She heard nothing that would provide her with the insight she needed. There was nothing here that suggested where Guya might have gone.

A part of her had hoped Guya had simply gone into one of the taverns, as unlikely as that might be. It wouldn't be like him to disappear like that, just as it wouldn't be like him to leave Dara behind, as sick as she was. But after all the time spent on the ship, maybe he'd only needed to get away for a while.

And leave Dara?

No. That wasn't Guya.

Something else had drawn him off—or else he'd been attacked—but what?

They reached the other side of the tavern having nothing that gave her any sort of insight. She let out a frustrated sigh and set down her mug of ale, not surprised when Julie made her way towards her, bringing Carth another cup to drink.

"What is it, girl? You look like you can't find the answer you need," Julie said.

Carth should have been more careful with her emotions. She didn't need it to get out that they were looking for Guya, or that someone they cared about had gone missing. Conversations like that would only get tongues wagging, and she wanted nothing more than to remain hidden, remain discreet. Having others know that she searched would only lead to more questions.

"You think you're going to keep your secret," Julie said. "Most in the tavern think the same thing. Enough ale, and tongues start moving. We hear pretty much everything in here. Not much comes through the taverns we don't pick up on."

Carth glanced to Lindy. Was it possible that Julie might have an answer they needed?

"What sorts of things do you hear?" Carth asked.

"Oh, all sorts of things. Most of the time it's the orphans. They get out of hand at times, stealing for the guilds. Then the excitement dies down and the council forgets about them." Julie shrugged. "Other than that, there's word about disappearances, but those have been going on for years."

"What sort of disappearances?" Lindy asked, leaning forward.

Julie shook her head. "The kind of disappearances you should be careful of. Too many been taken off the streets and sent… well, sent other places."

They thought she might say more, but Julie left them.

Carth glanced over to Lindy, frowning as she did. "Is she talking about slavers?"

Lindy shrugged. "I don't know these lands. I don't know what takes place here. Do the slavers make their way through here?"

From Guya, Carth knew they did. She also knew how Guya had felt about slavers. He had some history with them, though she wasn't entirely sure what it was. He had been angry when he'd discovered his ship had been used for slaving. That was part of the reason she had come to trust Guya so much.

They drifted toward the back of the tavern, where the music played. One musician carried a large stringed instrument, and another played some sort of lute. A third, a young woman with curly raven-colored hair, sang in a warbly voice that pierced the din of the tavern.

Carth and Lindy stood silently, simply observing for now. This wasn't the first time they had come to taverns together, searching for information. Lindy had been with Carth often enough that she understood what was intended. Finding information was often about listening, sitting back and letting the conversations swirl around her. It was how Carth intended to get a flavor of Asador and learn what she could about rumors she'd heard on the sea.

Pulling on the shadows, Carth used them in a subtle way to shrink backwards, not quite disappearing, but fading in a sense. She included Lindy in this, though the woman used her own connection to the shadows to help her fade as well. This was a technique Lindy had taught her, one that Carth had mastered. Others would still be able to see them, but they wouldn't necessarily notice them.

Lindy nodded to her and slipped away to listen to other conversations.

Carth remained where she was and noted a table next to her filled with armed men. Maybe she could find more than what Julie had shared. Most of the men at the table carried swords, but two wore crossbows hooked to their belts. Having a sword of her own—one she had trained to use were the need to arise—made her more comfortable in this strange setting. Leather helms rested on the table, in front of them three men dressed in thick leather, a kind of armor Carth had not seen in the north. The table was covered with mugs, most of them empty. She noted the nearest man slurring his speech. He propped his head on his fist as he talked, and his eyes had a glazed appearance to them. Two of the others shared a similar expression.

She hesitated. Sometimes intoxicated men would provide her with information. Other times, the intoxication would prevent them from saying anything of use. It all depended on the degree.

"Nothing moving through here the way it used to," the drunk said.

Carth could tell he spoke to the heavier-set man sitting next to him. That man had thick jowls and small, squinty eyes that somehow still seemed to manage to take in everything around him.

The squinty-eyed man shook his head. "Quiet."

The drunk one laughed with gusto. He looked around him, his gaze skipping right over Carth and

Lindy, pausing at the door before returning to his heavy friend. "What's there to be concerned about? No one knows we're here. Any who would know—"

The heavier man beat the table with his fist, drawing the attention of the intoxicated one. His eyes cleared for a moment, almost as if hammering on the table had shaken away some of the intoxication.

"This isn't the place to talk about such things. Too many others have an interest."

The drunk nodded slowly and returned his attention to the mug in front of him.

Carth glanced at Lindy as she returned to her. There was potential there, though it could be nothing more than smugglers. They'd encountered dozens of smugglers in dozens of different ports in their travels. All of them had a similar paranoid nature to them. Often, they seemed affable on the surface, but beneath the surface they possessed concern and uncertainty. What they needed was someone with deeper ties to the city; then they could find answers.

"Towards the back," Lindy whispered.

Carth let Lindy lead her, not certain what the other woman might have observed, but having learned long ago that Lindy possessed talent in picking out critical pieces of conversation. They weaved their way through the tavern, navigating around tables in between different groupings of people, both of them remaining hidden within the shadows. Lindy brought her towards the back of the tavern, surprisingly, leading her towards the musicians. She nodded at the singer, who continued to sing in a soft voice, one that had a haunting quality to it. She sang in a language Carth didn't recognize, but the words carried all the emotion needed.

"Do you recognize what she's saying?" Carth asked.

Lindy shook her head. "I've not heard that before, but there's something about her that concerns me. I don't know quite what it is." She glanced at Carth, meeting her eyes with a soft intensity. "It's mostly a feeling I have. We need to help her."

They watched the musicians playing, and Carth realized what it was that troubled her. There was an almost sedated quality to the woman, as if she had been dosed with something. It was evident in her glassy eyes as she looked around the room, and was likely the reason for the haunted quality of her voice.

When they finished, the musicians hurried away, forcing the woman to the back of the room and then out the door.

Lindy looked at Carth. "What do you think that was about?"

"I don't know. Not Guya."

"Not Guya, but it's something."

Something. Not Guya, not as they needed, but it was something. Carth only wished she knew what that something was. They were in a strange land, and she knew they had enemies here. The Hjan existed in these lands. And her friend was missing.

She needed answers. Would helping this woman bring her closer to those answers?

"What do you want to do?" Lindy asked.

Carth stared at the doorway. "I think we find her first, then we find out what happened to her..."

"How do you expect to do that?"

"The same way we looked for Guya and Dara."

Carth hoped they'd have better luck than they had so far in searching for Guya.

CHAPTER 6

THE AIR OUTSIDE THE TAVERN HAD A STINK TO IT. THIS was the smell of water that had been left standing for too long. It took a moment for Carth to realize that it wasn't water, but something else, like the decay of rot. Even that wasn't quite right. This was an unnatural sort of odor, one that didn't fit here—or anywhere, really.

Lindy stood on top of a box, peering down the street. She held her shadows wrapped around her, and without Carth's own connection to the shadows, she doubted she would have been able to see the way Lindy held her own connection to the shadows. The other woman stared intently, and every so often, she would motion to Carth.

"I don't see anything," Lindy said, stepping down from the box. Somewhere distantly, a cat meowed.

Lindy chuckled. "I've heard that some in these lands are superstitious about such things."

"She couldn't have disappeared," Carth said. "I still detect her."

"I think you scared her."

"I didn't scare her. They pushed her out."

Carth didn't know why, but she had a sense the singer needed help, though they didn't have any way of finding her. If she'd disappeared down the street, there wouldn't be any way of following her, at least not easily.

"Let's go back inside the tavern," Carth said.

They started around the outside of the tavern when they caught sight of motion.

Carth grabbed Lindy's wrist, stopping her. The two of them sank into the shadows, fading into the darkness. They waited.

Carth could slide with the shadows, but she didn't think Lindy could. That was a difference between being shadow born and shadow blessed, one of many.

A male voice drifted through their shadow cloaking.

"Where did she go?"

Carth glanced to Lindy. Had they been followed?

There was something coarse—and angry—about the voice.

"We've got to find her and bring her south. That was the whole reason we came through here."

"She can't have gone far. Not with what we gave her."

"You were responsible for watching her."

"I did. Something spooked her and she ran. Like I said, I'll find her."

Carth eased off her connection to the shadows enough to see the two musicians from the tavern hurrying along the street. They searched for something—likely the singer. Had she managed to get away from them?

She trailed them, and Lindy came with her. They remained in the shadows, hurrying along the street. If the singer needed help, they would be there to offer it.

One of the musicians twirled a knife as he walked. He had quick hands, not surprising given his skill on the instrument. In the taverns she had visited over the years, she had always known the musicians to have the fastest hands. Often they weren't paid as well as they should be either, making such skills necessary.

The men stopped at an alley and hurried along it. Carth paused, listening.

"There you are," one of the men said.

"I—I don't want to be here."

It was the singer. Her voice was tentative, and clearer than it had been in the tavern. Lindy started to step forward when Carth grabbed her arm.

"We should listen first," she said.

"It doesn't sound like she wants to be with them," Lindy said.

"Probably not, but we should get all the information we can before we act."

"Please. I just want to return to my home. You have to understand that."

One of the musicians laughed. It was a dangerous sound. "You have to understand that we have a job to do."

"Why make me do this? Why force me to sing?"

"Force? You enjoy this. And besides, how else are we going to find a buyer for you?"

Carth's heart started pounding and she began to pull on power. These men had abducted this woman and now they sought to sell her?

That was more than she could tolerate.

"Be ready," she said to Lindy. "When I give you the signal—"

She didn't have a chance to finish.

Lindy pulled on her arm, spinning her away from the alley to face three men that had appeared along the street. Carth hadn't seen them coming. Two of them carried swords. They were the kind of men she'd seen on the docks, the kind who had a dangerous sort of attitude about them.

Her focus on the musicians had distracted her. At least Lindy had not been so distracted.

The lead man leered at her, his eyes sweeping lazily over first her and then Lindy. "Looks like we found ourselves some entertainment for the evening," the man said.

He had a slight slur to his words, but Carth couldn't smell the stink of liquor on his breath. She wondered whether he really had been drinking or if he had taken another substance. Guya had warned that there were intoxicants besides ale popular in Asador.

Carth shook her head. She pressed out with a hint of shadows, pushing the men away with the power of the shadows. "I don't think you want to make that mistake." She glanced toward the alley. Were the musicians still there? Could they reach the singer in time?

The lead man grinned. "A feisty one. That's exactly the kind of entertainment I want tonight. I always enjoy it more when the woman fights."

She looked along the alley. She couldn't get distracted, not if the singer needed her help.

It was empty.

The men had taken her.

Carth doubted she would be straightforward to find. It would be easy for three people to hide in a city the size of Asador.

The heat of anger surged in her. Carth knew that she could leave, that she didn't need to fight, but it was men like these who turned into men like the blood priests. If she left them, would they harm someone else?

Men like this were like the musicians.

"Cloak yourself," she told Lindy in a hushed whisper.

She felt the shadows shifting and knew that Lindy had done as she had asked.

Carth took a step forward. "I think you're mistaken, but if you think that you could have some entertainment tonight, I'm also afraid that you've found the wrong kind of entertainment."

She unsheathed her sword in a rapid movement and spun, sweeping it towards the man. She didn't intend to strike him, wanting only to scare him, and used the edge of her blade so that even were she to catch him, she wouldn't harm him too much. She had little qualms about subduing him.

The lead man acted slowly, but the other two with him were not quite as slow.

With a flash, Carth detected the glint of metal. Both men unsheathed swords and formed two points on either side of her, but they did not appear accustomed to fighting together.

The lead man grinned. "See? I told you I would have my entertainment."

Carth considered using A'ras magic, or even reaching towards the shadows, but she hadn't had a good spar in months. When she had trained with the A'ras, they had sparred regularly. After losing the singer, she wanted to make these men suffer.

She decided to face these men unpowered. If nothing else, *she* could be the one to have some entertainment for the evening.

She slashed, feinting towards the first man before

withdrawing and spinning, coming around and catching the second with a quick attack.

The second man seemed to have expected her and he blocked, their blades clashing together. Carth spun away, turning towards the first again, sweeping her sword in a short arc, controlling it as she did, and the sword was caught by the other man.

They were good.

These were well-trained swordsmen, though not accustomed to fighting together. She was alone, with only her sword, with which she was not as skilled as she was with the knives, and she did not want to risk Lindy.

As much as she didn't want to, she pulled on the shadows, sliding towards the first man and wrapping bands of shadow around him. The slight tension around the corners of his eyes told her that he struggled. She struck him on the top of his head with the hilt of her sword, and he crumpled.

Carth began to spin, a sharp pain burning through her back. She almost dropped her sword, but managed to complete the movement and lashed out with shadows, striking the other man. He fell as well and his sword clattered to the stones. The third man, the one who had wanted nothing more than entertainment, turned and ran.

Carth staggered forward. Pain burned through her.

The sword had been poisoned.

She reached through her mother's ring that she still

wore and pulled on the power of the flame. With that, she sent a surge of heat and flame through her.

The flame magic allowed her to burn off most toxins and had healed her on more than one occasion. She used that power and felt it fill her. As she took a deep breath, the pain receded, replaced by the pain from using the power of the flame. When she stood, the other two had both recovered enough and looked up at her. Carth lashed out, kicking at both of them in a swift movement, each on the side of their head, and they fell unconscious.

Lindy released her connection to the shadows, becoming visible once more. "Well... that was interesting."

CHAPTER 7

"MAYBE IT'S TIME WE RETURN TO THE HEALER," CARTH said. The street carried the stink of the city, and a hint of blood from their attackers. She looked along the alley and didn't see any sign of the singers—or of the musicians. They had used the distraction to get away from her. "I think it's time we see if Dara is any better."

"We've only been gone a little while."

"Long enough," Carth said. Leaving Dara alone any longer made her uncomfortable, especially after what they had seen.

It was late, which meant it was early in the morning, and Carth wondered how much longer it would be until the sun started rising above the horizon, casting away the shadows of the night. Lindy glanced to the sky at the same time, likely having some of the same questions.

They wandered through streets that were much emptier than they had been before, making their way towards the healer. By the time they reached the yellow door, the sun had begun to rise.

They should've long since been asleep, and had they still been aboard the *Goth Spald*, they would have been asleep long ago. If not for Dara, they should have spent the night looking for Guya.

The door was once again locked, and this time when they knocked, no one answered. Carth was unsurprised given the early-morning hour. She unsheathed one of her knives and pressed this into the lock, twisting it back and forth until the lock popped open.

"Is that really necessary?" Lindy asked.

"Necessary or not, I want to see if Dara is any better. We can pay for any damage done."

"That's not the issue," Lindy said as they entered, but she went silent as they reached the inside of the healer's shop.

Both noted that it was different than the last time they'd been here, and the time before. Dark scorch marks marred the floor. The contents of shelves were spilled, and the scent of medicines, that of spices and herbs and fresh cuttings, hung in the air.

"What happened?" Lindy asked.

Carth made her way back towards the cot but found it empty. As she pressed through her mother's ring, reaching for the flame magic, she probed for others with the same power. The scorch marks suggested that S'al magic had been used, but why?

As she feared, she detected a faint power in the air. The S'al magic had been used here, and dangerously so. That meant Dara had awakened. Had Dara used her power?

If so, why? What would have made her need to use her power, and expose herself to the healers? And why would there have been such a struggle?

"Where is she?" Lindy asked.

Carth breathed out, surveying the entirety of the healer's shop. "I don't know. Missing."

How was it that both Guya and Dara were now missing?

The sun was fully up by the time they returned to the *Goth Spald*. Carth stalked toward the ship and didn't hide her abilities as she jumped on board, not waiting for Lindy to follow. Frustration and anger mixed together as she returned to the ship.

A part of her hoped she would find Guya here, and that he would answer why he'd disappeared, but she knew better than to think he had returned, just as she knew better than to think Dara might have returned.

As she feared, the ship was still empty.

Nothing had changed about the ship since they had left, and in the daylight, the trail of blood left by Dara was even more pronounced. How could she have missed it so easily at nighttime?

Carth went below deck and noted the pile of vomit outside Dara's door. There was probably something she could discover by sifting through it, but she had no interest in studying the vomit. She entered Guya's room once more and grabbed the pile of books, thumbing through them, but no answers were to be found there. The room was otherwise empty.

Lindy had followed Carth down and gripped her dress in a clenched fist. "What happened to him?"

"I don't know, but it's time we find answers."

Worse, she didn't know what had happened to Dara. She *should* have been safe at the healer's shop. Carth would return there and find answers, but first she needed to make sure she was fully armed.

Carth checked her knives and the rest of her supplies. Lindy did the same. Fatigue was threatening to catch up to her, and her eyes were heavy and tired, but now wasn't a time she could sleep. Now was the time she needed to search.

But where to start? Carth knew so little about the city, she didn't even know where to begin looking for answers. And maybe there were no answers. In a city the size of Asador, people could disappear and never resurface. She had seen it happen time and again in Nyaesh. Men would come off ships, disappear into the city, and never be heard from again. The only way others knew was because they looked for them, searching for answers as to what had happened to them.

Like what had happened to the singer.

Carth vowed not to let that be Dara's fate.

CHAPTER 8

Carth moved along the street, keeping quiet as she went, remaining draped in shadows. Days had passed since losing both Dara and Guya, precious time that made it increasingly unlikely that they would find them. It frustrated her that she couldn't find Dara, and that she had lost Guya, essentially leaving her struggling to discover what else she needed to do. She didn't know enough about the city to find her friends, but it wasn't the first time she'd visited unknown cities.

So far, her experience in Asador had led her to believe that there was an undercurrent of violence here. It was similar to what she'd experienced in other places, but this made her uncomfortable. She had the ability to use her shadows, and she had the ability to draw upon the flame, but she didn't have the control necessary to use her talents and discover where her friends had gone.

She made her way along the shore, listening to the sound of the waves crashing. Lindy had gone off on her own, searching for other information, thinking that one of the two of them would discover answers. In the city the size of Asador, there were always people willing to provide answers. The challenge was always in discovering who knew them.

She and Lindy had already explored the taverns, looking for something that might be hidden there, but so far, they had not discovered anything useful. There were rumblings, an undercurrent of something taking place, but she knew nothing more than that.

Dara was bad enough, but losing Guya seemed surprising to her. He wouldn't have simply abandoned his ship. The *Goth Spald* was more important to him than anything else, especially as he had already nearly lost it once before when his second-in-command had betrayed him. Carth suspected there was a connection between Guya's disappearance and the healer, but the shop had been empty each time she had gone there for answers. She decided that it was possible the woman had abandoned it.

Without the taverns for assistance, she decided to look in other places, searching for a hint of the underground. In cities like Asador, there was always a connection to the underground. She wasn't certain how to reach it—not yet—but she was determined to find it. Then she could get answers to what happened to both Dara and Guya.

One thing that Carth had was the ability to observe. She could shield herself in the shadows and watch and listen, and with that connection, she thought she could find the answers she needed.

The docks were always a good place to observe. In Nyaesh, that had been the best location for her to collect scraps, thieving from men coming off the ships, but there were others there who were even more deceptive and traded in things other than scraps. There had been the Thevers, men who were part of a dangerous cabal, and they had access to information that others did not.

Would there be something similar to the Thevers here?

She suspected there would, especially as they were known to smuggle across the sea.

A man pushing a cart appeared along the shore, and she followed him. It was late to be moving goods, probably too late to be anything other than someone doing so illegally. The man turned off the road heading along the shoreline and made his way toward a more run-down section of the city.

That surprised her. She expected that he would have disappeared to the north, where there were large warehouses, but he didn't. Along this road, there were smaller shops, and eventually it changed over to homes. Carth could see those buildings from the *Goth Spald*.

Another man joined him.

Carth remained hidden in the shadows, staying quiet. The two men didn't speak for a while until the newcomer whispered, "You shouldn't move so openly."

"What's open about this, Cason? All we're doing is walking."

Cason grunted. "If the guild finds out—"

"And how would the guild find out?" The other man smiled at him. "I'm not going to say anything. Besides, I doubt you have much of value."

"Enough to get their attention."

"What are you moving?"

"Ceramics."

The other man laughed. "Ceramics? What kind of market do you think that has?"

"There's a market for all these things. Otherwise they wouldn't be on the ship."

"Sometimes your captain just gets too caught up in what he thinks might work without thinking about what he can actually move."

"Has it ever not worked?" Cason asked.

The other man fell silent, and they continued along the street. Carth debated whether she should continue following him. This was a smuggler, which wasn't what she needed. She needed answers and doubted that she would get them from some low-level smuggler. What she needed was somebody deeper in the underground.

Maybe what she really needed was to return to the taverns and see what secrets she could hear there. Men always talked in the tavern, and if there was anything going on, she would discover it there.

She sunk into the shadows and turned away, leaving the two men walking along the street.

There came the sound of a distant scream, and Carth hesitated.

As she often did, she felt compelled to react, but that wasn't what she needed to do now, was it?

There came another scream; this time it was silenced quickly.

It was close. Close enough that she might be able to react.

Wasn't that the other reason she needed to be in the city? She couldn't abandon someone else who might need her, not if there was something she could do to help.

Sighing to herself, she turned down the street and raced toward the sound. There weren't many people out at this time of night, and those who were never saw her passing as she remained hidden within the shadows. She raced onward but didn't hear any additional sounds, nothing that drew her as the last scream had.

Had she missed the opportunity?

Shrouded as she was, she heard the sound of hushed voices whispering.

There was a sense of urgency to them, one she had recognized before.

Carth ran toward that sound and found two men dragging someone between them.

Grabbing her knife, she leapt forward, surging on the power of the shadows.

When she reached them, she kicked one of the men, and he spun around to face her. He had a plain face, but hard, dark eyes. He reacted quickly, unsheathing a sword.

The other man didn't hesitate and dragged the other person off, flipping them over his shoulder before racing along the street. Carth couldn't give chase, not until she dealt with the man holding the sword in front of her.

"You might do nicely as well," he said. "They've asked for those with spirit."

"Who are they?"

The man sneered at her and slashed with his sword. She danced back, deflecting it with her knife, but she was at a disadvantage with the shorter blade. She needed to react differently, so she jumped, surging with the power of the shadows to slip up and behind him, and then she kicked, catching him in the back. He stumbled forward but righted himself quickly.

He swung his sword, forcing her back again.

He had reasonable skill with a weapon, though nothing quite like she had learned during her training in A'ras. If she had her sword, she would be able to more easily counter him, but she had only her knives.

Carth danced back, away from his blade, avoiding his attack. All she needed was one solid blow, and she could catch him, and hopefully slow him.

She slipped her knife around, slashing, but missed, and his sword cut deeply into her shoulder. Carth cried out softly and nearly dropped her knife. The man gave a satisfied smirk and lunged forward, attempting to strike at her more closely.

She jumped and surged the power of her flame through the injury and her shoulder, letting that magic lead her healing as she had in the past. It wasted strength and required much of her, possibly too much.

She had to stop him, and needed to find out what they had done to the person they'd carried off.

Drawing on the power of the shadows, Carth jumped, surging into the air and spinning as she did.

As she twisted, she jabbed down with her knife, catching the man in his shoulder and pinning him to the ground. He twisted, burying the knife more deeply into his shoulder.

Carth swore under her breath. That hadn't been her intent. Blood pooled around her hand where the knife had penetrated, and he stopped moving.

She withdrew her blade and wiped it on his shirt. That had not been the plan. As she sheathed her knives, she looked around, searching for the other man and the woman he'd carried off. She saw no sign of them.

She swore again, this time anger coursing through her.

She brought her hand up to her shoulder, checking to see how injured she was. The skin had already started to knit back together, the power of the magic sealing it once more. It still amazed her how quickly and easily that power could be used to heal her injuries. It amazed her that she had such magic that could repair her, restore her when injuries like that occurred. She could even heal herself from mild poisonings, though she didn't dare risk that too extensively, not knowing how the magic would work if she were to encounter something more significant.

Answers.

Carth thought about what she knew and tried to think through what she'd observed. Dara was missing, as was Guya. She had just seen a woman taken in the street—twice, she reminded herself—and she'd overheard conversations within the tavern of similar activities.

There had to be a connection.

But what was it?

Maybe Lindy was having better luck than she was. Carth hoped that was the case. If not, she didn't like to think about what would be required to find her. In a place like Asador, a place with ships coming in and out of the port and a place she knew to be home to slavery, she feared what might be taking place.

Answers.

She needed them, and she thought she knew how to find them, but it might involve taking a harder edge than she was accustomed to.

For her friend, wouldn't she do that?

CHAPTER 9

THE INSIDE OF THE SPOTTED LION WAS DINGY, AND RUN-down. It was situated in the center of the row of taverns lining the docks. A simple wooden sign hung from chains, consisting of nothing more than a few letters burned into a board.

Carth had observed the tavern for a long time before choosing to enter. It had the look of the kind of place that she thought might provide answers. Those taverns had a distinct appearance about them, one that she had grown comfortable with during her years. Few women would be as comfortable as she was entering the tavern like that, especially alone, but few women were Carth.

There was a ribald air to the tavern. A minstrel played a stringed instrument in one corner, and a dozen people danced around him, some singing and some shouting, but mostly they simply danced. There was no real coordination to their movement, and she smiled to herself as she watched, thinking of discovering something like that in Nyaesh. She would not, she knew. The taverns there were places for eating, and gambling, but rarely for dancing, not like this place seemed to be.

Those other activities took place here as well. At several tables, she saw men dicing, and at another—one in a corner—four men sat hunched over a table with a game board situated across it, moving stones along the surface. It reminded her of Tsatsun, but it was not the same. Would it be similar enough for her to pick up the gameplay quickly?

These were the kind of men she needed to find, the kind of men she thought she would get answers from. They were the kind who would have access to the underground.

Others moved through the tavern as well. Much like where she'd met Julie, there were three different women who made their rounds, carrying platters laden with ale or trays of food. The smells coming off the food made her mouth water, and Carth didn't know if that was a sign of her hunger, or whether it reflected the quality of the food. Probably the former. The meat had a grayish appearance to it, and the vegetables were all overdone.

One of the serving women—a rounder woman with wide hips and a plentiful bosom—cast a strange glance at her as she entered. Carth shrugged and turned her attention to the game board in the far corner.

Dicing was a game of chance, one she had played often enough in other taverns in other cities, but with her abilities, she could overwhelm the chance and could force things in her favor.

Where would she get the most useful information? That was of the utmost importance to her now. She wanted to hear gossip, but she also wanted to hear what else might be taking place, so that she could understand where to make her next move. Each step needed to bring her closer to information about what had happened to Guya and Dara.

Carth probably should have done this from the very beginning. It was a tavern like this—perhaps not quite so filthy and run-down—where she had first convinced Guya of her skills. That had been after she'd rescued him, dragging him back to shore after he'd been betrayed by his first mate. That had been the start of them working together, and Carth learning how to sail, finding comfort in moving from port to port. As she'd never really had much of a home in the first place, traveling on board the ship seemed natural to her.

For gambling, dicing would have been the easier of the two. But Carth didn't want to gamble. She didn't need the coin. Her coin purse was heavy enough the way it was. What she needed was information, and that was something men more deeply into the drink could provide.

She surveyed the tables with men dicing before settling on one. There were two younger men, and a third slightly older, sitting there.

Carth grabbed a chair, pulled it up to the table, and rested her elbows. The men all glanced at her. "This isn't a place for women," the older man said.

She scooped the dice from the table and shook them, rolling them with enough energy so that Watcher's Eyes came up, both an unlucky hand and a lucky one. She shrugged and flipped a coin that she'd palmed onto the table.

"Then why are you here?" she asked with a smile.

The man sputtered, but his friends both laughed, one of them covering his mouth with his hand as he did.

Carth had been around taverns often enough to know that there was a certain measure of insult needed to handle men like this. Coming up with the right thing to say to him wasn't difficult. In fact, it was entertaining.

"The game is closed," the man said.

Carth tapped on her coin, drawing attention to it. "Closed? That's unfortunate. I thought you might want to show this poor woman how to gamble."

The man sitting across from Carth took the dice off the table and shook them, rolling them out. He rolled a five and a six, a healthy hand, one that was difficult to beat, especially if they were playing based on total roll. Not all played the game that way, and Carth wasn't certain which set of rules they followed. She suspected that dicing was different here, and from the time that she had diced with Guya—at least, *for* Guya—she had discovered there were different rules for the different types of dicing in different locales.

The man reached for her coin, and Carth slapped her hand on top of it. "We haven't agreed to anything."

"I thought—"

Carth shrugged. "You thought, but first we agree to the game, then you can try to take my money."

The two younger men who had been dicing before she'd arrived glanced at each other, and then the one nearest her shrugged his shoulders. "What does it matter? We can take her money the same as we could take anyone else's."

Carth smiled to herself. That was exactly the kind of attitude she wanted from them. If they believed that they could take her money so easily, she could sit back and let them.

"We dice like men," the older of the two said to her.

Carth slipped her hand into her pocket and grabbed a few of the coins in her coin purse. She shook them in her hand. "Really? Then perhaps you should prove it, and stop talking like women."

She grabbed the dice and shook them in her hand. "What's the game?" She continued to shake the dice, curious about what they might prefer.

"Highs," the man nearest to her said.

"Out of how many?" Carth asked.

The two men glanced at each other before shrugging to each other. "Three?" the nearest one to her asked.

The other man nodded. "Three is probably safest."

Carth only shrugged. She shook the dice and spun them across the table. In a game like this where the highest hand won, she made no effort to augment her role. Doing so would only draw suspicion on the first hand. Instead, she let them roll without influencing them.

The dice came up with a four and two fives. It was a good roll, but not one that would draw attention. With the roll like that, she could sit back knowing that she would likely lose her coin, but less concerned about that than having an opportunity to sit back and listen, observe what these men might say while dicing.

The other younger man grabbed the dice, shook them, and spilled them onto the table. He came up with two threes and a six.

The other man grabbed the dice from him, chuckling to himself. "A shame, but looks like I'll be taking your coin."

He shook the dice, and when he spilled them on the table, came up with a three, five, and a six. He let out a satisfied holler and reached for the coins. Carth didn't make a face and simply slipped another coin onto the table, pushing it to join theirs.

The man who'd won grabbed the coins, and shook

them again, making a satisfied face as he did. "Twins or higher."

"Do you really want to risk that? You've seen how many doubles I've rolled," the other man said.

"You? You barely rolled any. Last one doesn't count, since you lost the hand."

"It counts. Don't make me reach across the table and grab what's mine."

The other man grinned and spilled his dice across the table. They clattered before coming to a stop. There were no pairs. He swore softly to himself while the other man grabbed the dice and scooped them up. "Not such a bad roll now, would it be?"

He shook them and came up with a pair of twos. Carth glanced at the two men, debating. Was now the right time to push it? Would she draw too much attention by rolling a hand that would beat a pair of twos?

The better question was whether she cared.

She did, but maybe these weren't the kind of men who would discuss matters within the city while dicing. They seemed more content to joust with one another, and not at all concerned about anything else.

Maybe dicing with them wasn't the right play.

She still thought they were the right men to get her what she wanted so that she could learn about the underground in the city and find a way to access it, but maybe it wasn't exactly the way she had initially intended. Carth rolled, pushing the dice so that two fours came up. She smiled and shrugged as she reached for the coins.

The older man grabbed her hand and tried to pull it back, but she pressed a bit of shadows through it, resisting.

His jaw clenched with the effort he exerted in trying to move her hand. "The hand's not won."

Carth kept her hands on the coin, knowing this kind of man. She'd seen men like him before. "No? Seems to me that three of us were dicing, and three of us rolled. It seems to me that my fours were higher than his twos. Unless you understand numbers in a different way than I do, I think that makes mine the winning hand."

"I didn't get a chance to toss yet."

The other two men glanced at each other, but neither spoke.

Carth kept her grip on the coins and simply shrugged. "Throw your coin in, and let's see what you toss." He glared at her, but Carth ignored it until he set a coin on the table. When he did, she removed her hand and waited for him to pick up the dice. He did so, but with a certain reluctance.

Carth smiled to herself. This was the kind of man who sought to control the flow of the game, which meant this was the man who ran the other two.

He shook the dice, and they clattered across the table, coming to a stop slowly. Carth gave one of the dice a little push. It was enough to send it teetering, toppling so that the pair that he might have rolled were unsettled.

She wasn't above playing the same sort of games with him that he attempted to play with her. She wasn't above doing it to draw attention to him.

When the dice stopped moving altogether, he glared at them, as if expecting them to move again.

Carth felt a hint of pressure on the dice but it was subtle, and she thought it imagined.

Could he have some ability that would allow him to control the dice?

That opened up different possibilities, and raised more questions.

Had she overplayed her hand? If he did possess some ability, it was possible he would pick up on her influence, but she got the sense from him that this was not a man who was aware of any sort of subtlety.

Carth grabbed the coins and slipped them into her pocket.

"Maybe next time you'll dice like a man as well," she said.

The other two men both grinned. "I like her," the nearest man said.

"Fine, you keep dicing with her. Lose all the money you want."

He eyed Carth in a way that made her think that he recognized what she had done.

He wouldn't have picked up on that, would he?

The man stood and disappeared into the crowd near the back of the tavern.

Carth watched him go, debating how much to push. Had she already pushed too hard?

It was possible that she had, especially as he had seemed the one in charge. Then again, she wanted to irritate the man in charge so that she could discover what role he might have.

"Is that it? One hand?" one of the men asked.

Carth turned her attention to him and smiled widely. "Only if you want to keep your money."

CHAPTER 10

Outside the tavern, Carth hesitated, remaining in the shadows. She'd taken quite a bit of money from the two men, even more when it became apparent that neither of them seemed willing to talk about anything going on in the city. Remaining here seemed a waste. What she needed was to find answers, and she apparently wouldn't find it from either of these two men.

But… she thought that she could draw them out. She could annoy them, and in doing so, she could see whether they could be baited into sharing more information, but what else could she do?

Carth waited, hoping that one or both of the men would appear outside the tavern, and would reveal something that she might have missed before. Maybe they would talk between themselves, and she could see what more they knew, though from the conversation they had—one that seemed mostly about which women in the tavern they most wanted to bed —she wondered whether they knew anything useful at all.

She felt movement behind her and started to turn when she heard voices. The two men were intoxicated, all the ale they had drunk while playing with her had having gone to their heads, and they staggered along the street. Every so often, they would bounce off each other before somehow managing to right themselves and then continue onward.

Where was the third man?

Carth suspected she would see him, but he had not emerged from the tavern. Then again, she might have already missed him when he'd come out.

Did she follow, or should she wait, looking to see where the third man, the one who had to have been their leader, had gone?

The men neared the end of the street, and she hesitated to wait too much longer.

She didn't know why, but she felt compelled to follow these two. Maybe it was only a familiarity. Maybe she could coax one—or both—into talking, and sharing what they might know about the underground within Asador. Or maybe it was simply the fact that she'd overheard enough from them that it made her question whether they knew more.

Pushing off with the shadows, she jumped and managed to leap past several of the buildings and into the distance, far enough that she could hurry along in the shadows and follow the men from enough of a distance that they wouldn't know that she was there.

As she approached, she could hear them still talking about the waitresses from the tavern. Did they have to be so disgusting talking about the women that way? Why was it that so many of the men in taverns believed that they could treat women as if they were nothing more than something to grope?

Not all were like that. Guya was respectable, and he had been angered by the slavers, something she had appreciated about him. Then again, not all men could be like Guya.

She needed to find him. If anyone could help her navigate the underground throughout Asador, it would be him. Maybe she needed to stop focusing on trying to find Dara and trying to understand what else was taking place within the city, and instead she should work on seeing what had happened to Guya, and where he'd gone.

That was a question she *could* ask.

Carth hurried through the darkness, keeping the shadows wrapped around her, and as she approached the two men, she slowed. She readied herself to step out of the shadows when another figure approached, reaching them from within the alleys.

"Where is she?"

It was the man from the tavern, the third gambler.

Carth cloaked herself, wanting to avoid him realizing that she was there, and that she was watching.

"She left. She took our money, and she—"

The man slapped him, cutting him off. The sound rang in the night, a sharp *crack* that stood out from the other sounds of the night. "She took your money and you let her go? Didn't you wonder why she was there?"

The two men glanced at each other. "Why was she there?" one of the men said. Carth couldn't tell which it was from here, not that it mattered. To her, both men were basically one and the same.

"How many women did you see in that tavern?" the third gambler asked. "Doesn't strike you as odd that she was there, that she came to a place where no others were willing to go?"

One of the men shrugged. "Does it matter? She came in and wanted to dice. Anyone's allowed that."

"Not there. And I think there was something more than chance about the way she won."

The men both laughed. "There's only chance when it comes to dicing."

"Chance? It sounds like she won more hands than chance would allow. Why do you think that is?"

"Eric, it's only chance."

The third gambler—Eric—shrugged. "Maybe that's all it is. Or maybe, there's something else. Remember what Terran said. He wanted to find those with potential. And seems to me that a woman who can win at dicing"—he glanced between the two men—"and often, might have something special to her."

"Aw, Eric. Let's not bring Terran into this."

"If you didn't want to bring him into it, then you shouldn't have spent so much time dicing with her."

They started off down the street, and Carth let them go. There was no need for her to follow them now.

She had a name.

CHAPTER 11

THE TAVERN WAS MUCH NICER THAN THE SPOTTED LION. The music was upbeat, but not so loud as to be over-bearing. She tapped her foot as she sat inside the tavern, waiting for the woman she anticipated to appear.

Lindy sat across from her, chewing on her lip, her hands clenched beneath the table. Carth didn't need to use her abilities to know that Lindy's agitation came from a lack of information that she discovered. She had searched and come up empty. That troubled Lindy as much as it troubled Carth.

"What if she's not here tonight?" Lindy finally said, breaking the silence between them.

"She'll be here."

She wanted to find Julie, feeling a hint of connection to her, nothing else. She trusted Julie, and trusted that she might learn something from the woman, that she might have answers for her.

With a sigh, Carth surveyed the tavern. She pressed out with her connection to the shadows and added to that a hint of the flame, wanting only to see what she might detect. And maybe there would be nothing. Maybe Julie would be hidden from her, but if she had answers, they would have a place to start looking.

The door to the kitchen opened, and Julie popped out. She carried two trays, one on each hand, and navigated through the tavern with a confident air to her. As she approached, she noted Carth, and her face clouded slightly. She made an effort to turn away, weaving as if to move back toward the kitchen, to get away from Carth, but Carth leapt from her seat and blocked Julie from disappearing.

"I'd like to talk to you."

"I don't need any trouble here," Julie said.

Carth looked around the tavern. It wasn't particularly busy tonight, and she couldn't see anyone who might be watching, but what would trouble Julie?

"Trouble?"

"I've heard about you. You bring trouble with you."

Julie had heard? That bothered her. "Just a word. That's it."

The woman let out a frustrated sigh. "Why did you need to come back here?"

"I didn't need to. I chose to. Be thankful of that." Carth guided her back to the table where Lindy waited.

Lindy stood and allowed Julie to take a seat, which the woman did reluctantly. She stacked the trays on top of each other and folded her hands on top of them.

"What do you want?"

"I want to know who Terran is."

The corners of Julie's mouth twitched. It was subtle, but it was enough that Carth realized the woman recognized the name. "You know who he is. I can see it."

Julie controlled her breathing. "Even if I did, it will do me no good to tell you what I know. All that will happen is others getting hurt."

"Why? What is it that you fear from him?"

She shook her head slightly. "Fear? I fear the same as any woman in the city fears."

"And what is that?"

"Attracting his attention."

"Well, I might have attracted his attention. Tell me why I should be concerned."

Julie glanced from Carth to Lindy. Her fingers twisted as they rested on the two trays. "Like I said, I don't need any trouble here. Let me continue to do my job, and continue to work. I don't need Terran to come into the tavern looking for me. That's the kind of attention I've avoided. Don't bring me into whatever it is you intend to do in the city."

Carth fixed her with a hard-eyed stare. "What I intend to do in the city is find my friends. It seems that there is more taking place than what you or anyone else would tell me. From the moment I first get off the ship, I'm practically attacked, and now you tell me that you're terrified of some nameless man."

"Not nameless. You have his name. You shouldn't, but you do. I would suggest that you choose not to say it—at least not too loud. Doing so will only attract his attention. As I said, I don't want that kind of trouble here."

Julie started to stand, and Carth grabbed for her wrist and pulled her close, forcing her to bend down and look at Carth and meet her gaze. "Who is he? Why are you so scared of him?"

Julie cast her gaze around the tavern before turning her attention back to Carth.

"I can help. I'm not completely helpless," Carth said. "Tell me who he is, and I will do everything I can to ensure that he doesn't harm you."

Julie laughed bitterly. "Do you really think I care so much about myself? I'm not worried about him coming after me. Well, maybe I am a little. But I'm concerned that he'll come here, and take others I care about away from me." Her eyes drifted before settling on a woman near the far corner.

Things started to come together for Carth. There was singer from the first night, the one she had been unable to help. There was the other woman grabbed on the street when Carth had nearly died. And there was the fact that Dara was missing.

She doubted they had anything to do with Guya,

but the fact that all these women were missing—and the way Julie seemed terrified of this man finding her —told her that she must have somehow discovered the slavers' ring.

She had known there was one in Asador. Guya had shared that much with her. But where did they take these women? And how did they get them out of the city without anyone else noticing?

"What does the city council do about this?"

Julie face clouded. "There's not enough money to purchase the kind of protection we need."

"Is that how the city works?" Carth asked.

"That's how every city works."

Carth glanced to Lindy, who nodded. "Not the ones where I am."

Julie grunted. "What do you think you can do? Do you really think you can stop him? That you can break up the chain of women being dragged from the city?"

Carth nodded. "I do. As I said, I'm not entirely helpless."

"Then may the gods watch over you. I'll pray for you when you're dragged someplace south like Eban or Cort. Not that that will do any good."

Carth sighed. This was not a woman who would help. This was a woman who was scared, which was something that Carth had experience with. She hated that places like this existed everywhere. What she'd seen in the north had been bad enough. Now she was dealing with something very similar here in these lands.

It frustrated her. More than that, it angered her. She wasn't entirely helpless. She would do what she needed to do to get help to Dara.

"Help me," she said to Julie.

Julie looked around before focusing on her. "I don't know how to find Terran, but I know a man who might."

"If you know that much, why can't you stop him?"

"Because those who have tried either have not returned or have died."

"They're not the same?"

Julie pulled her arm away. "They're not the same. Sometimes death is better."

CHAPTER 12

CARTH CROUCHED ALONG THE SIDE OF THE STREET, THE shadows wrapped around her. She envisioned Lindy doing something similar not far from her but couldn't see her. There was the subtle work of Lindy's shadows, the faint effect of their swirling, bending to conceal her, but nothing more than that.

They needed to find this Terran, as he seemed like the only person who might have answers about what had happened to Guya. She suspected that what had happened to Guya and what had happened to Dara were related. She didn't know quite *how*, and that was what she was determined to understand.

As the hooded man emerged from the tavern, she trailed him, flowing with the shadows. Julie had said this man worked with Terran, and she would follow him until she had the answers she needed.

He hurried away from the tavern, occasionally

casting his eyes up and down the street, and when he did, she sank deeper into the shadows so that his gaze swept past her.

At first, he seemed to go toward the docks once more, and Carth wondered if perhaps she had missed something along the docks, if maybe there was another ship there that had abducted the others. As he neared the water, he turned, taking a different path than what Carth had expected. Now he veered north, heading along a different street, one that took him into the smaller and quieter sections of the city.

Here, there were rows of homes, the roofs not quite as peaked as they were near the center of the city, most of them in various states of disrepair. At this hour, not many people moved. The man in the hooded cloak hurried through the streets, and Carth began to feel hope that she might be able to find her friends, but the farther the man went, the less certain she became.

He didn't stop as the houses began to space out even more. He didn't stop when the terrain transitioned into nothing but hard rock. He continued north, taking a narrow trail leading toward rock leading over the edge of a cliff leading to the sea, hurrying forward quickly. Either he had some way of seeing in the dark or he had been here often enough that he didn't need light.

Carth had to slow to make her way through here, weaving around the rocks as cautiously as she could, afraid of stumbling and falling. She heard the distant crashing of waves, and the air grew thick with the scent of the sea, that of salt and something else that she thought might be more imagined than real.

She saw no one else moving along this way.

Carth circled around a particularly large rock, and when she popped up, there was no sign of the cloaked man.

She eased back on her connection to the shadows. How had she missed something? Where had he gone?

He couldn't have simply disappeared. Were he able to flicker—travel, as the Hjan called it—she would have expected him to have done it by now. And she was attuned to that flickering, and could feel it as a nausea in the pit of her stomach when it occurred. There had been no such sensation.

She continued to make a slow circle, looking for evidence of where he might have gone, but still she saw nothing. Somehow, he had disappeared.

But where? There wasn't any place he could have gone here. There was nothing but rock and the sea.

Swearing under her breath, she knew it was time to return to the city.

As she turned, she noticed a shifting of darkness, a sign of motion. Carth readied shadows and flame but was too slow. Something heavy struck the back of her head and Carth crumpled.

When Carth awoke, her head throbbed.

She reached for the shadows immediately. She could touch them.

What of the flame?

As she reached for it, it burned through her. The flame was not kept from her either.

Her hands were bound together with thick coils of rope, and her legs were similarly tied. The heavy cloak she'd taken to wearing had been removed, and her knives taken from her, but she still had her mother's ring.

At least she was dressed, if only in her underclothes.

Carth looked around and saw a small, compact man with flat blue eyes almost the color of ice staring at her. His hair was shorn close to his scalp, and he had a long thin nose that flared as he breathed. His lips were parted slightly, as if in a frown or a snarl.

"Why did you follow my man?"

Carth sat up and scanned the room. It was all of simple stone. A single lantern sat on the floor in the corner, casting a flickering orange light. She tested the ropes and found they were tied to her tightly. With her connection to the flame, she suspected she could escape, but this was an opportunity more than it was anything else. If these were the same men responsible for Dara's disappearance, she would find out.

"Where am I? Where did you take me?"

The man pulled out a long, curved knife and set it on his lap. Carth's gaze flicked to the knife, noting the unique style. She hadn't seen any fashioned quite like that before, and she could see value in its deadly form.

"Why did you follow my man?"

Did the man even know who he had captured? Did he know that she could escape, or that even if she could not, she could harm him? Unlikely. If had he known, they would have killed her and never have brought her in.

"A friend of mine is missing. I wanted to see what happened to her."

"You're not from Asador, are you?"

Carth considered whether to be honest with him, or to conceal where she'd come from. She didn't know enough about the lands in the south to effectively fabricate her story, but she suspected that were she to admit coming from the northern lands, if they did have Dara and Guya, she would reveal herself sooner than she intended. As in so many things, it felt much like playing a game, playing the right move, but needing to determine her strategy.

"I'm not from Asador. I'm from Balcath," Carth said, thinking of a distant enough island that wouldn't be too far off the coast of Asador. At least she had visited Balcath and knew she could provide enough details of it were she questioned. It would potentially explain her fair complexion, perhaps even the darkness of her eyes compared to most she saw around here.

The man swept the knife across his legs in a way that she suspected was meant to be threatening. Carth let her attention be drawn to the knife, knowing that he would expect that of her. When she looked up to his face, he smiled.

"Who's your friend?" he asked with twisted expression.

"She came from Balcath like me. She's not well. We brought her here for healing." Most of that was true enough, and would provide enough details that if they did have Dara.

She *would* find her.

The slight tension in the corners of his eyes told her that he recognized the description, as vague as it had been.

"She's a lovely one," the man said. "A shame for her, really, especially as she caught Terran's eye."

Carth had known the name, but this confirmed it. It was disappointing that *this* man wasn't Terran. "Why would Terran take her?"

"I think you'd be better served not worrying about your friend. She's been added to the collection, and you have been added to mine."

Carth decided it was time to get real information from him.

With a surge of A'ras flame through the ring on her finger, she sent heat through the rope bindings around her wrists, and they burned off in a flash. She did the same with the ones around her ankles.

Gliding with the shadows, she leapt, flipping over

her captor, grabbing his knife as she did and quickly bringing it to his throat. He tensed beneath her grip.

"I think it's time we have some answers."

She checked him for additional weapons but found none. Up this close to him, all she could smell was his stench, and he disgusted her. This was a man who thought to *collect* women.

She threw him across the room, where he collided with the cot and stumbled onto it. He looked over to her with a wide-eyed gaze, meeting her eyes rather than looking to the knife she clutched in her hand. It was a strange sort of weapon, one that she only now noticed had spikes along the hilt that pierced her skin.

She felt a surging, steady sort of burn through her, slowly working from her fingers up into her arm.

She had made a mistake.

Carth slumped to her knees, pain surging through her arms. She reached for the power of the S'al, trying to draw on the strength of the flame, which had healed her before.

Pain made her focus difficult.

She sent it coursing through her, but she didn't have the necessary strength to use it in a way that would overwhelm the poisoning from the knife.

She looked up, noted the man staring at her, nothing more than simple curiosity on his face. She'd mistaken his casual interrogation for some sort of incompetence. He might not have any magical power, but he had not been unprepared.

As the poison worked up her arm and into her chest, burning as it did, she reached for the shadows, trying to draw them around her, to give her one last burst of strength, but even they failed her.

The man stood, the grin parting his lips as it had before, and he nodded to himself. "I think you will make an excellent addition to my collection."

Carth sank to the ground, unable to say anything more.

CHAPTER 13

WHEN CARTH AWOKE, SHE WAS TRAPPED. SHE REACHED for her connection to the shadows, and then attempted towards the S'al, but failed with both. Her mind had a fog over it, and she struggled to bring her thoughts into focus. She remembered the poisoning, but not much else.

Could she move at all?

She rolled onto her side. That movement required all the strength she could muster. Carth wiggled her fingers, then her arms, bending her wrists and her arms, testing her shoulders and neck, before moving onto her lower half. All parts seemed to work.

Though they worked, she felt weakened. It was as if her strength had been leached away from her. Her connection to her magic had been taken from her, and not the way it had been when Ras had abducted her.

Had this been the first time she had been powerless,

she might have reacted with panic. Instead, she took stock of herself.

Carth noted narrow slats with light leaking through. There was a sense of movement, a steady swaying sort of movement, unlike anything she'd ever experienced before. She lay on the floor of some sort of closed wagon.

There were others in there with her, all girls of various ages. Few of them bothered to look in her direction. Those who did didn't let their gaze linger for too long.

Carth sat slowly, assessing those she was with. She saw no bindings. She realized she had none herself. A few of the women had a glassy-eyed sort of stare, one where they fixed their eyes ahead blankly, almost as if intoxicated.

They must be dosed with something to keep them incapacitated, but what?

It was hard coaxing her mind into action as she tried to think through the fog. If she was here, could Dara be with these girls as well? She didn't see her, but that didn't mean that she wasn't in this room or another.

She licked her lips, and her mouth felt dry and sticky. When she worked moisture back into her tongue, she leaned forward, trying once more to reach for the shadows and, when they failed, to reach for the power of the flame. Neither worked.

"Where am I?" Carth asked.

None of the women looked in her direction.

Carth frowned. Why wouldn't they at least acknowledge her? Were they so scared to answer? Or did they fear her?

"Where am I?" she asked again.

Two of the women sitting along the benches towards the middle glanced her way, but neither said anything. The rest simply stared.

The answer dawned on her slowly. They weren't scared of her. They were scared of their captors.

She tried forcing her mind to think through what she knew, but it was difficult. She recognized the connection between what had happened with Dara and the fact that she was now captive. The man who had captured her had recognized Dara. She remembered that much. He had said a name... what was it?

The name came to her slowly, like surfacing from a great depth. Carth grabbed for it, struggling to hold the name in her mind, but knowing that it was important for her to do so.

Terran had been his name.

That was all she had. A name. The reason she was here, chasing after information regarding that name. There was nothing else, no other way of pursuing him, only the name and the fact that Dara was missing, but more than missing. She had been added to the collection. She remembered that term as well.

The thoughts were coming easier. She licked her lips, hoping that if her mind lurched forward, that meant that perhaps her magic would return to her as well. Each time she tried accessing it, she failed.

The movement stopped, and she staggered forward. A door opened that she had not noticed before, and bright sunlight spilled inside. She shielded her eyes and instinctively tried to remain patient as she waited to see what might be coming for her—for all of them— but struggled to think of whether there was anything more.

A face appeared in the doorway, one she recognized. It was the man who had captured her, who had taunted her.

No… that wasn't it.

He hadn't taunted her; he had allowed her to reveal her abilities. She remembered sitting in the room with him, bound with ropes at her arms and legs, until she had made the mistake of severing that connection. Had she only been more patient, perhaps she would've allowed him to reveal himself, and the fact that he possessed a poisoned knife.

That had been Ras's warning to her. She always had a tendency to act a little too aggressively, taking the fight towards her opponent as opposed to waiting and letting the game come to her. Ras had used that tendency. Carth knew that now was not the time for her to act impulsively. She needed patience, even when that patience might be difficult.

"Come on, get out."

The man's gaze swept over the women before

pausing on Carth, and a smile spread across his face before he turned away, leaving the flash of sunlight once more streaming into the enclosed wagon.

The women began filing out, one after another, moving in a practiced sort of motion. None of them spoke, none of them did anything other than follow their captor's instructions.

They had been through this before.

Carth understood the look she'd seen on the women's faces. Maybe it wasn't entirely the look of someone who was drugged or intoxicated. These were the faces of those resigned to their fate.

What did this man intend for them?

He had referred to a collection and stated that he was going to add Carth to it. She knew that slavers moved through Asador, and she knew there was likely a connection to them, and to what had happened to Dara. She still hadn't learned what connection the slavers had to Guya, if any.

And Lindy... she was alone in the city now, not knowing what had happened to Carth, likely worried that the same thing had happened to Carth as had happened to Dara and Guya.

When it was Carth's turn to exit, she hesitated. She felt stupid for allowing herself to get captured. This should not have been her fate. She was too powerful, too strong, and too skilled at playing these sorts of games to have allowed herself to be captured.

Except... she wasn't.

When she stepped free from the back of the wagon and into the sunlight, she saw the women all standing around, none of them making an attempt to run. There were only two men standing outside, one of whom was the one who had captured her. The other was a slightly older man, one whose face wore the signs of previous battles, scars marking his cheeks and neck. He had a clean-shaven jaw and narrow slits of eyes.

She glanced back and noted a second wagon behind hers.

Could Terran be there?

If it was, maybe that meant Dara would be there as well.

Anger started seething through her—and not only for herself and for the stupidity with which she had let herself be captured. As she looked around at these women, she felt anger at what had been done to them.

It was no different than the way the blood priests had attacked the villagers along the shores. They had used them, used the women. The men in the south were no different.

As the two men swept their gazes over the congregated women, Carth made a quiet vow to herself. She would get free.

There was no question in her mind of her ability to do that. She had been trained by the A'ras, and even without her magical abilities, she had skill in hand-to-hand combat and was not helpless. But these other women, those who had already given up, those who appeared to have resigned themselves to their fate, those were the women who needed her help. Women like the villagers who had been taken by the blood priests. She would not allow harm come to them.

But first… first she must be patient. She needed to understand what was happening here, and when she did, then she would act. Then she would destroy not only her captor, but all those who worked with him.

His gaze settled on her, his eyes a flat blue that matched the sun in the sky. She wondered if he knew her thoughts. Carth made no expression. And when the women were motioned towards a barrel of water, Carth followed them, cupping her hands into it the same as they did, drinking freely of the water, moistening her lips, all the while not taking her focus off her captor.

She would destroy him.

CHAPTER 14

THE CARAVAN MOVED SLOWLY OVER THE NEXT FEW DAYS. Carth felt the steady swaying from the wagon, her mind remaining in some sort of haze, and she struggled to form coherent thoughts, only able to maintain the desire to see the flat-eyed man injured. Every time they stopped, the women filed out of the wagon, and she followed with them.

They usually went long enough in between stops that her mouth was incredibly thick and dry, with her tongue feeling bloated, so that she eagerly consumed the water she was given. Meals consisted of meager portions of dried meats and occasionally lumps of bread. The flat-eyed man, whose name she had discovered was Lothan, forced the women to prepare the meals on a routine basis.

Carth hadn't taken a turn at preparing meals, but she watched the other women as they did, and noted that most worked without saying a thing, mindlessly following the directions of the two men who led the caravan.

Every so often, her mind cleared enough for her to feel a renewed surge of anger at her situation and what these men forced the women to do. She felt helpless, impotent to do anything more than simply observe, hating that she was not able to reach the powers buried within her.

Even with her foggy mind, the memory of using the flame and the shadows never faded. Each time she attempted reaching for them, that power seemed to skirt away from her.

Carth lost track of days.

They had traveled for more than a few days but not much more than that, though she couldn't keep track. Her focus was on following the commands of the wagon drivers, and obtaining the water and food with each stop. The one time she'd attempted to avoid drinking, she had begun retching.

Remembering what had happened to Dara, she hurriedly took a small sip of water, thinking that if nothing else, she didn't want to get dehydrated.

She still hadn't seen Dara.

Would she recognize her if she did? Had it been too long already?

During one of the stops, as she waited in line for her turn to drink from the bucket of water, she had a flash of a memory and began thinking of the *Goth*

Spald. What had happened to the ship? With Guya, Dara, and now her missing, what would Lindy have done? She couldn't have managed the ship on her own, and Carth doubted she would've attempted to.

She sipped the water, letting the cool, clear liquid run through her fingers, and let herself forget about what might be happening with the *Goth Spald*.

It didn't matter.

Nothing mattered other than getting free of her captors, finding what they did to poison her, and discovering if there was some sort of antidote.

At times, she attempted conversation with the other women, but they rarely spoke to her. A few times they would acknowledge her presence, but more than that, they seemed to prefer staying engrossed within their own worlds, as if anything Carth might do would disrupt the tranquility they had with their silence.

Every so often in the evenings, one or two women would be brought off the wagon, and they would disappear. Carth hadn't learned where they went, and most of the time they returned, saying nothing.

One of the nights, a woman disappeared and did not return.

Carth waited throughout the night, thinking that she must have been assigned a chore like cleaning the cook site, helping to tend the fire, or any one of the other half a dozen tasks that they were given in the night, but the woman never returned. At one point in the overnight hours, she thought she overheard voices, but it came through something like a fog, drifting to her consciousness almost as if more of a dream than something real.

When the woman didn't return the following day, no one seemed to mind, and no one seemed to say anything. It was as if her absence were not remarkable. How many others had been like this?

At first, that troubled Carth, but the more time passed, the more she began to forget about it, and began to forget about the fact that anything was amiss.

On a night after she'd been assigned to assist with the fire, tending it to ensure logs were tossed carefully onto the fire, making sure that the flames built properly and the heat maintained a consistent warmth, Carth was called from the wagon in the middle of the night.

The door opened, and moonlight streamed in.

There should be something about the moonlight that drew her, but she didn't recall what that was. A strange chill was on the air, and she shivered, wrapping her arms around herself.

A hooded figure met her at the doorway, and she recognized the face of the flat-eyed man. He motioned to her, gesturing with that strange curved knife of his, the one that gave her chills each time she saw it. That seemed important, but why would it be?

Carth stood, her body aching and joints creaking as if she were older than she thought she might be, and she made her way towards the open doorway, not certain what tasks she might be assigned this evening.

One of the women did look up at her then. She eyed Carth, her mouth pinching into a thin line, and as Carth passed, she touched Carth's hand, squeezing her fingers almost reassuringly. Carth lingered longer than she should have, and the flat-eyed man reached into the wagon and grabbed her, pulling her out.

Once out of the wagon and back under the moonlight, Carth wrapped her arms around herself, fighting against the chill in the air, blinking to clear the haze that hung over her mind, knowing that she should be able to think more clearly, almost able to remember a time when her thoughts didn't require such effort to drag from the back of her head.

The flat-eyed man watched her, waiting as if she might say something, but when Carth never did, he motioned for her to follow him.

Was she going to be like the women who'd returned, or was she going to be like one of the women who hadn't? Worse, she didn't know the difference between the two and what that might mean for her.

They followed a trail from where they camped for the night. It led through a grassy plain, with trees visible to her in the distance. Shadows flickered at the edge of her vision, brought on by the moonlight, almost as if she could feel where they began and ended. Cool air carried a hint of dust and earth along with a threat of rain.

There was something about the moonlight that was important. Or was it the shadows? She wished she remembered why.

When the flat-eyed man stopped, Carth noted some lights in the distance. Was that a village? A city? Maybe that was the destination where they brought them.

She opened her mouth to question, but the man smacked her across the face, as if anticipating the fact that she had intended to question him.

Carth bit back her reaction.

But the strike *had* done something.

It had created a boiling anger within her.

Heat surged within her, as if her blood boiled with anger. With the heat and the anger, her mind started to clear.

She remembered.

This was the man who had abducted her when she had sought to learn what had happened to Dara.

And what of Dara? Did they have her?

She couldn't recall seeing Dara with either of the wagons, but given the way her mind had been working, she wasn't sure she would remember.

Carth considered attacking, but she needed an answer.

Why had this man brought her here tonight?

It was tied to whatever their reason was for abducting her. And the more her mind began to clear, the more she began to suspect that it was related to the same horrible reasons that women had been abducted from Asador for countless years. It had been bad enough when others had been the ones taken, bad enough when she had done everything she could to help save them, but this time it was her.

It was personal in a way that it had not been before.

She would wait. And then she would make her move.

She didn't have to wait long.

Another man appeared, emerging from the darkness, from the shadows that she should be able to reach but could not. As he did, he glanced from the flat-eyed man back to Carth, as if appraising her.

"This is the girl?" the newcomer asked.

The flat-eyed man nodded. "You'll like her. She's spirited, which I believe you said you sought. You'll need to work with her, and it will take some time to break her, but I have no doubt that you'll succeed." He held out something in his hand, and the moonlight reflected off a vial of a powdery substance.

Carth frowned. Was that the reason her mind was so foggy? If it was, how did they manage to continue doping her? She didn't recall being drugged, unless it was in her food. Or… the water.

What a horrible way to drug the women. It would work, too, especially given that she suspected the side effect of the drug was the dry mouth she now had. Why wouldn't they immediately reach for something to drink, a way to rinse out the cottony sensation in their mouths, and to quench the thirst given to them by the drug?

Anger boiled within her even more strongly.

Carth recognized it this time for what it was. It was the power of the S'al magic burning within her. It strained to escape, but more than that, it strained to help release her from the captivity of the drug.

The newcomer nodded again. "Spirited. Yes… I like spirited."

He had a slickness to his voice, almost as if there were an accent she weren't able to place. Though she had traveled the north extensively, she didn't know nearly as much about south and wouldn't recognize the accents of this land.

"And she won't be recognized in Cort?" the man asked.

The flat-eyed man shook his head. "She won't be recognized. All of my girls are brought away from places they might be recognized. You'll be safe. Claim her as your wife, claim her as your mistress, or claim her as your sister. No one will question."

Carth wondered if this was what had happened to the other women, and if so, whether some had returned.

Had they been brought out like this for a bargain that had never occurred? Had there been another intent with them? Had something else happened when they were brought out from the wagon?

Carth wanted to attack, but with no weapon, she

had no way of ensuring that she would be able to succeed.

Her mind continued to lurch forward. She hadn't been thinking clearly for some time. How long had she been poisoned?

If she escaped now, she could likely free herself, but there were others who were a part of that caravan who needed help. The women might've stared at her with their blank expressions, but they would not have known any way to find freedom, perhaps not knowing whether such a thing were possible. That didn't mean they wanted to remain captives.

That meant Carth needed not only to get free, but to find a way to reach for her powers. Once she did, she thought she could attack and could rescue them.

After that, she could discover what might have happened to Dara. Maybe she was there. If not, the rescue still needed to happen.

Besides, the flat-eyed man seemed to know something. There was a reference to a man named Terran. That would be where she started.

The best move in this game was keeping her mouth closed. Then she could attempt to escape.

The buyer stepped forward and peered at her, grabbing her cheeks between his thumb and first finger and pinching, twisting her face from side to side, almost as if studying her like she was some sort of animal. And to a man like this, she suspected that she was. To him, she was probably no more than another slave.

Anger surged through her once more, but she kept it contained within her. She would not react; she would not do anything that would endanger her ability to find freedom. But that would take patience, and patience had not always been her strong suit.

But… she couldn't risk being *too* patient. Were she to be lax in what she planned, the caravan could escape, pulled by horses that could move faster than her. What would happen were she to lose sight of it? She didn't know where it headed, and even if she had, she didn't know these lands well enough to know where to find it. That meant dealing with the buyer quickly enough that she could return and follow the wagons.

She flicked her gaze to the cloudless sky and the moon. She had the night.

The buyer seemed content with what he saw, and he stepped back, reaching into his cloak and pulling out a thick purse that clinked as he tossed it to her captor. The flat-eyed man held the purse open, flicked his finger through it as he seemed to count the coins within, and once content, he tied it closed once more and pocketed it.

A dark thought came to Carth's mind. What was the value of a woman like her? Did they know that she had access to magic as she did? Would that have made her more valuable? Or was it only her spirited nature that made her more valuable?

Those thoughts sickened her, as did the idea that the same transaction had happened many times before.

She had thought that the women would've been sold openly, and was relieved to know that such trade was not welcomed throughout the south. It was a relief to know that such transactions had to be done stealthily, and under the cover of night.

In many ways, Carth appreciated that the transaction happened at night. At night came the shadows, and with the shadows came Carth. The shadows were hers, and it was time these men began to understand that.

When her buyer grabbed her wrist to lead her away, she did not resist. She glanced at the moon again, noting the time she had remaining, and wondered if she would be able to break free and return to the wagons before the morning.

Would she be able to do so?

CHAPTER 15

As her buyer led her away, Carth whimpered softly, hoping to convince this man of her fear. She needed him to think her subdued, needed him to think that she would be afraid of something worse happening to her.

And she was afraid.

She feared what he intended for her. A man like this, a man willing to purchase a woman and turn her into a slave, likely using her in some sort of horrible way she could not imagine… what would it take? What sort of thoughts burned inside his brain to allow him to do something like that to another person?

The man stopped and jerked on her wrist. "You will be quiet as we move through the night. I see that he's struck you before. Do not think I will be any less forceful."

Any hope that this man might be somewhat reasonable, that he might not have interest in harming her or treating her with the same disrespect as the flat-eyed man had treated her, evaporated with that comment. That gave her all the answer she needed as to what sort of man he was, and took away any hesitancy she might've had about treating him with violence.

"I only want to go home," she said with a whisper. She tried pitching it in such a way that she would be believable, that he would think that all she really wanted was to return to her home. If only she had a home. The *Goth Spald* was her home.

"You're with me now."

He grabbed onto her wrist and dragged her forward. Surprisingly, he didn't lead her towards the lights in the village. He brought her towards a narrow path that wound through the tall grasses, leading towards the dark smear of trees in the far distance. Curiosity stayed her hand and prevented her from attacking him. She didn't know if he had any weapons on him, but she suspected she could incapacitate him before he could react, and that she could get free fairly quickly. Partly, she wanted to know where he was taking her. She had time, likely several hours from the angle of the moon as it moved through the night sky, but not enough to be too complacent.

When they reached the trees, Carth noted two other men.

She swore to herself. She'd missed her opportunity.

Had she attacked before, she would've been able to escape. Now she had to contend with three men.

If she had access to her magic, or even to her knives, she wouldn't fear the odds. As it was, she was at a disadvantage.

The longer she walked with the anger still boiling within her, burning through the poison the flat-eyed man had used on her and the other women, the more she began to have a clear mind.

She still could not reach for her powers and knew that was intentional. But why?

What was it they used on her that prevented her from accessing those abilities? Even with Ras, when he had captured her, he had not separated her completely from the flame or from the shadows. She had been able to reach them but had not been able to use them against him.

The fact that she was completely separated from them now, that she could not reach them, scared her more than anything else. She might have a clear mind, but she did not have the resources she was accustomed to.

The man stopped near the other two. Carth noted that three horses were saddled near the tree line. Horses were rare in the north, but she'd seen them more commonly in the south, and the wagons had been pulled by four horses each, lumbering along, pulling the wagons with them, moving at a pace she would not have been able to maintain had she been marching alone.

One of the men, a smaller man with a hooked nose and eyes that barely reflected the light of the moon, stepped forward out of the tree line. He wore a short sword on his belt, and he moved with a grace that spoke of comfort using his weapons. This was a man to watch, a man she knew she would need more than only her knives to confront safely.

"Why this one?"

Her buyer glanced back at her. A dark sort of smile twisted his mouth. "They called her spirited."

"Spirited? What does that mean?" the smaller man asked.

The third, larger man, who in some ways reminded her of Guya with the way his arms bulged beneath his shirt, muscles even rippling beneath his pants, stood with his arms crossed, watching them wordlessly.

Her buyer chuckled. "Spirited because they don't know what they had. They never know. That's why they dose them with slithca syrup."

At least now Carth knew what they had used. The man pulled the vial of powder from his pocket and shook it.

"They mix this with water. Less potent that way, but it would be tasteless, and it has the added advantage that it would remove any potential from those with it."

"This one doesn't appear to have any potential."

The man shot Carth an interested look. "No, she

does not. But this was the one he said was the most difficult capture. The most difficult capture is often the one who has the most potential."

"Spirited?" the smaller man asked.

The other man nodded again. "That is what he said."

What had happened here? What had she gotten herself into?

These men seem to know about different abilities and seemed unconcerned about the fact that she possessed them, not even worried about what those abilities might be.

Who were they? How was it that they seem so unconcerned with the fact that she might possess some way of harming them?

She felt conflicted. Here she wanted nothing more than to return to the caravan, rescue the women, and kill the flat-eyed man so that she could reclaim her knives. At the same time, she wanted to understand who these three men were, and discover what they might know about her and whether they might know of others like her.

"Where did she come from?" the smaller man asked.

Her buyer grabbed her by the cheeks again, pinching her face in his strong grip. Carth chose not to fight, knowing that doing so would only reveal herself to him now. As far as he knew, she was still drugged. She wanted him to think that for as long as possible, needing to use that to get the advantage.

"Look at her dark hair. That's not the southern trait.

Light skin as well. I think she's from one of the northern isles. I'm not sure which one, but once we get her talking, she'll share."

"The north?" the smaller man asked. "Where would they come across somebody like that?"

"You know all the ships that come through Asador. Likely they grabbed her off a ship, thinking her nothing more than a courtesan. They have weird customs in the north."

The large man opened his mouth and grunted out his response. "Strange powers, too."

The other two men looked to him, and both of them nodded. Her buyer spoke. "Yes. And strange powers. That's why we have her. Whatever power she possesses, we need to understand. We can use that power." He nodded to her. "Bring her along."

Were they with the Hjan? She didn't think so. They didn't appear to have the scars she associated with the Hjan, and none of them had moved by the strange flickering movements that Invar had referred to as traveling. Yet… what else would they be?

"How far are we going to get tonight?" the smaller man asked.

Her buyer glanced from Carth to the horses. He frowned, and then, with a motion so swift she didn't see it coming, he struck her on the back of the head, and she crumpled.

CHAPTER 16

CARTH AWOKE TO EARLY-MORNING LIGHT, A GRAYISH sort of dawn spreading through the trees. The horse swayed beneath her and she feared toppling off it, but somehow did not.

Her head throbbed, and it angered her that she had now been knocked unconscious twice in a short period of time of time, both times by men who had not seemed to have any sort of special power or ability. Here she had thought herself so powerful, and so clever after learning to play the game Tsatsun, but she had been bested more than once by men who should not have bested her.

Trees rose around her, and the smell of pine and thick wet earth clogged her nostrils, letting her know that she traveled through a forest. With the growing light of day, she knew that she had been out too long, long enough that her goal of reaching the caravan, rescuing the women, and destroying the flat-eyed man was no longer possible.

A plan formed in her mind—one in which she stole the horse and escaped from these men, possibly killing them as she went—before she dismissed it. She had no ability to ride a horse.

Still, she needed to escape. That much she did know.

Her mind remained clear, something that had not been the case when she had woken from her captivity with the flat-eyed man.

Another horse rode alongside her. The buyer from the night before leaned towards her face, and in the light of day, she was able to see the way he studied her. He had dark brown eyes and hair to match, and a more youthful face than she would've expected. In spite of that, his expression was hard, and she knew he was accustomed to getting what he wanted. This was not a man for her to overlook. This was the kind of man who led another deadly man like the one who carried the sword.

Whatever else happened, she would have to be careful.

She reached for the shadows and felt a flicker, almost as if she could touch them, but then they faded from her, slipping free from her grasp.

Carth bit back an angry swear under her breath. She shifted her focus, trying to reach for the S'al that burned within her, but unlike the night before, it no longer came to her.

The man smiled slightly. "If you think to reach for some sort of ability, know that they would be limited. I have given you slithca. Do you know what that is?"

Carth shook her head and then stopped because of the throbbing within it. Her head ached from where he had struck her. "No," she croaked.

"Most with abilities in the south recognize slithca. This confirms my suspicion. Where are you from?"

"Balcath." Carth used the same island she'd used before. It would fit his expectations, far enough north that she *could* have been from there.

Her captor cocked his head. "Balcath? Your complexion is far too light for those of native to Balcath. And your speech doesn't have their usual inflection."

He leaned forward and grabbed the sides of her face once more, pinching her with that hard grip of his. Carth clenched her jaw, wanting to say something, wishing for the strength to resist, to fight, to strike back. She hated the fact that her magic failed her.

"Where are you from?"

"Talun." She would let him think she was from anyplace but Ih-lash, or even from Nyaesh. If he had heard of either of those, he might know the nature of her magic, so that when it did return—and she was determined to see that it did return—he might have some way to counter it, much like Ras had been able to counter her.

It was bad enough that he had given her some sort of drug while she had been unconscious that prevented her from reaching the magic. It would be worse if they could do that as well as counter it were she to regain the ability to reach it.

"Talun? They have a particular marking they place upon their children." He grabbed her arm and yanked up her sleeve, before doing the same thing with her other arm. A smile spread across his face. "Not Talun. Not Balcath. You have an accent unlike any I've ever heard. I hear hints of Salosh and Yinr, but it's not what I would expect. I would guess that you are well-traveled, but with a woman your age, I would not have expected such travels. Tell me, where are you from?"

His tone had grown harder the more he spoke, and Carth felt a flutter of fear in her chest. Anything she might say might be misconstrued, but worse, she suspected he would know if she did not tell the truth. This was a learned man, one who recognized nations in the far north, to the point where he recognized small details that Carth had not even known. A scholar? It was possible that he didn't really know, but more likely was the possibility that he *did* know. And if he did know, it wouldn't be long before he discovered where she really was from. It was all the more reason for her to conceal it as long as possible.

"Vichton," Carth said, naming a village that had

been destroyed by the blood priests. The village was no more, and there was no way to prove that she was or was not from Vichton. In addition, the village was so small that she doubted anyone would recognize it. If he did, she had another answer prepared. "My homeland was destroyed, and my parents moved us, trying to find a safer place. That's how I ended up in Asador." That much he could allow to be true. Let him think she had come here for safety. Let him think that she was unaware of her abilities.

Her captor's brow furrowed and he shrugged. "Perhaps you are. We will know soon enough. You won't be able to reach your abilities, though I wonder how much you know of them. Enough to make you—what was the word?—feisty. Yes, enough to make you feisty."

He left her alone then, leading his horse away from her, so that Carth rested across the saddle, her head still throbbing with every movement, questions racing through her mind.

This was no simple man. This was not someone who had purchased a slave for prostitution; this was something else. More than ever, she needed to know why, and who he was.

Still... she had to do so quickly, because she needed to get back to the caravan before it traveled too far. She had to get back to the caravan before another of those women were sold as she had been, before anything worse could happen to them.

And she still wanted to destroy the flat-eyed man.

CHAPTER 17

THEY REACHED A SMALL CLEARING IN THE FOREST, THE sun burning through the trees, and Carth was lifted off the back of the horse and thrown to the ground with no more concern than were she a sack of grain. She cushioned her fall, rolling to the side, but her breath still was pressed out from her as she landed.

She suppressed a grunt, trying to limit how much she revealed herself. Already she was concerned that the scholar who had purchased her knew more about her than she wanted. He had discovered enough in the few moments that he had spoken to her to make her aware that he likely would pick up on small details without her needing to share anything. It exposed her, making her uncomfortable in a way she had not felt when she had been captured by Ras.

Carth looked up through the trees, noting the fading light of day. She logged a count within her mind, keeping track of how many days it had been since she had been in the wagon. The longer she went, the less likely she would be able to return.

Find the flat-eyed man, find the wagons, and rescue the women.

She kept that chant within her mind, knowing that if she did not, those women would be sold and worse would happen to them.

Her buyer seemed to have no interest in harming her. He might have held her, and he might confine her, but he had done nothing to harm her so far. That didn't mean that he wouldn't change, or that he wouldn't strike her. She prepared for that possibility, knowing just how likely it was that he could change in a heartbeat.

The smaller man with the hooked nose threw a waterskin at her. Carth glanced at it, afraid to drink from it, especially considering that she thought that she had been poisoned when she had last drunk some water.

The man grinned. He picked up the waterskin and shook it. Popping the top off it, he said, "Just drink, all right? It's safe enough."

He took back the water bottle and took a long drink himself. When he replaced the cap, he tossed the water bottle at her feet, and Carth simply stared at it.

Her hands and legs weren't confined. They didn't seem concerned about possibility that she might run. Without any abilities, she doubted she'd get far.

She eyed the horses tied to one of the trees with an appraising stare. If she could reach one of the horses, she thought she might be able to untie it quickly, and... then what?

She wasn't nearly as skilled a rider as these men. She didn't doubt they would be able to chase her down with the other two horses, and without her abilities, without the potential to use either the shadows or the power of the flame, there was very little she could do if they were to recapture her.

Then again, she could fight hand to hand, and had been trained that way by the A'ras. Even a simple weapon, a knife or even a club, would help her even the odds somewhat.

The scholar came and crouched in front of her. He noticed the direction of her gaze and he grinned slightly, pushing the waterskin towards her. "I suspect you are thinking of how you could escape. I would be doing the same in your situation. Know that you won't be able to outrun us. You are here. I purchased you. You are mine."

"What do you want with me?" Carth asked. She kept an edge of steel in her voice. She wasn't going to let this man think he had her cowed or let him think he would bend her to his will. No... she would show that she could not be broken.

"Spirited. Yes. You're everything he promised. I think that you will do what I need soon enough."

The scholar stood and started away, stopping in

front of the large man, and the two of them talked quietly to each other. When they finished, the larger man did something with the horses, and Carth didn't have to stare too long to realize that the scholar had suggested he secure the horses more securely.

She rested back on the ground, letting her head make contact with the soil. She stared up through the trees, watching the night come along. How long would the poisoning hold? How long would they keep her here, constricted and separated from her abilities?

All she needed was a slight edge to escape. That was it, nothing more. If she could manage to get a moment where she could sneak away, she would have to. As much as she might want to know what they were doing and what they planned, a greater need weighed upon her, that of discovering where the caravan traveled now.

Carth took the water and glanced at it. She considered taking a drink, but what if it was poisoned like the other water had been? That seemed to be how they kept her abilities from her.

But they had to think that she was every bit as poisoned as she had been. If she could convince them... then she *could* escape.

She kept her eye on the scholar and took the stopper off the water bottle, tipped it up to her lips, and pretended to drink. When she was finished, she wiped her arm across her face, and set the waterskin down with the top loose just enough so that it would drip into the ground.

The scholar came over and grabbed the waterskin. Carth shifted her leg to cover the ground where she'd set it. He shook it, nodded to himself, affirming to Carth that it had been indeed poisoned. At least she knew that much. Now she would have to find a way to drink without subjecting herself to the same fate. That meant finding another source of water, waiting as the poisoning wore off.

Carth had time. She would wait. She had no other choice.

They didn't rest very long that evening. Carth slept fitfully, but she slept. She tried to keep on edge, maintaining her focus, knowing that she needed to in case they tried to sneak a different poison into her. For now, they believed she drank from the water bottle, but if that didn't last, if they started to question whether she really had, she wanted to be alert for the possibility that they might somehow sneak it into her. She wasn't completely sure whether the water was tainted, but she had enough suspicion to avoid it.

She awoke to the sounds of one of the men moving, his feet shuffling through the dried grasses, and she looked up to see the smaller man sneaking off, disappearing in between the trees. Carth stared into the darkness, wishing for the shadows to lessen somewhat, anything so that she could fade into them, or use her cloaking so that she could disappear.

It didn't happen, but her eyesight had always been good in the darkness, likely tied to the fact that she was shadow born. She noted how the scholar and the larger man rested, both of them lying on their backs, their breaths coming regularly, and even the larger man snoring softly. Neither of those two men knew the smaller man had disappeared.

What was he playing at? Was there something else afoot that she hadn't quite discovered?

She remained motionless, waiting, her eyes cracked just enough so that it would seem that she slept if he returned suddenly. She kept her breathing slow and regular, doing everything she could to mimic sleep patterns.

She lost track of time and might even have slept a little when the smaller man returned.

He came back into the clearing, his hands stained. Was that blood or something else? Then he took his place on the ground once more, resting near the others. It wasn't long before his breathing became regular and steady like the other two, the sign that he actually had fallen asleep.

Carth smiled to herself. If there was something more taking place, that might be her way in. She just had to find out what it was. Once she did, then she could start trying to play these men against themselves.

It was as good a plan as she could come up with.

―――――――

When morning came, Carth was still not fully awake. She struggled through the night, barely asleep, eyes snapping open at every sound, curious if the small man might disappear again. He never did. The scholar and the larger man woke first and began prepping the horses for departure.

Carth feigned sleep until it became clear that they knew she was awake. The scholar dropped the water bottle next to her, lingering a moment.

She glared at him, putting as much hot anger into the expression as she could muster, not sure whether she really convinced him.

She took water bottle, tipped it back, again pretending to drink.

This time, she set it on the ground, letting it spill out into the soft earth, before quickly placing the stopper back on it. The scholar didn't seem to notice. When he turned his attention back to her, she watched as he shook the waterskin and seemed satisfied that she had drunk.

They broke out some jerky and handed it around. Carth was less concerned with the jerky, as there didn't seem to be any way of telling a difference between hers and the others'. They likely shared the meat, making it less likely it was poisoned.

Then again, the smaller man had drunk from the water bottle.

But that had been meant to throw her off. She was certain of it.

Maybe it didn't matter to him. Maybe he didn't have any sort of abilities to suppress with whatever was in the water. The large man and the scholar had not attempted to drink from it. That mattered, somehow.

They rode through the morning. As they did, Carth sat stiffly in the saddle, trying to get a handle on how to ride. For her to escape, she would have to have control over the horse. It was a dappled gray mare and moved swiftly. She gripped the saddle tightly, probably too tightly. Each time she tried directing the horse, it seemed to fight her.

Escaping on horseback would not be easy.

The others rode more comfortably. The smaller man rode behind her and made no effort to touch her. In spite of the way she had been purchased, and in spite of the threats, she had been treated reasonably by the others. So far, she had not been harmed in any way.

She needed to get away, but she couldn't shake the strange curiosity that rose within her, trying understand why they had captured her and what they wanted with her.

She wasn't even sure what direction they traveled; the thick forest and travel by horse made it difficult for her to know. The canopy overhead shielded her eyes from the sun so that she couldn't tell in which direction it rose, only that it was sunny and bright. As the day progressed, they made no effort to stop, even at a narrow stream where the horses paused briefly.

Carth's mouth had begun getting dry, and she felt herself growing weaker from dehydration, but she refused to drink from the waterskin when it was passed to her several times throughout the day. Each time she pretended to drink, each time she spilled out a little bit more water, and each time they took the bottle back from her, seemingly content that she had in fact drunk from it.

She still could not feel the edge of the shadows, and she did not feel the fire burning within her that would announce that she could reach this the S'al flame once more. Yet, she was determined not to drink, insistent that were she to remain captive, she would discover a way to regain her abilities.

When they stopped for the evening, the larger man tossed the waterskin to her.

Even this task had been handed down, the scholar no longer concerned about her compliance. Carth feigned drinking once more, tipping the water bottle back, even letting a few drops run down her chin. She wiped her mouth with her sleeve and set the bottle between her legs as she sat on the ground, letting some of the water spill into the grassy soil. The large man grunted, and she handed the bottle back to him, not wanting to upset him. Like the other man, he shook the bottle, and left her alone.

When they sat down for the night, lying on the hard-packed earth, Carth pretended to sleep. She let her eyes drift closed but forced herself to maintain her attention. It wasn't long before she heard the soft and steady sound of snoring coming from the big man and regular breathing from the scholar.

She cracked a lid and noted the smaller man still lying there, but his breathing was too quick, and he shifted from time to time, making it clear that he was still awake. It wasn't long before he slipped out, disappearing into the night once more.

She should remain here, listening. Waiting. Eventually, the poison *had* to wear off, didn't it?

But that wasn't her.

Carth tensed before impulse brought her to her feet, and she followed the other man out into the trees.

CHAPTER 18

CARTH TRAILED AFTER THE SMALLER MAN, HIDING behind the trees as she went, moving carefully, but finding stealth in the shadows. A part of her mind told her that she should get some rest, and she definitely *shouldn't* attempt to run, but she ignored it as she maintained a steady pace, following the smaller man as he disappeared, and moving steadily away from the camp.

Where did he go?

This was the second night he had snuck away. She had thought him firmly with the others, but the fact that he snuck away like this made her question whether he was.

His step slowed as he went, and she moved more carefully, maintaining her position behind a large trunk for longer and longer periods of time before continuing onward. He didn't seem to follow any sort of path, as if he knew where he was going.

After a while, they emerged near a large, hard-packed road. The trees parted around them, giving room for the road to move through the forest. The canopy overhead parted and shadows swooped down from the sky, letting some of the moonlight filter through. She heard an owl hooting, and the wind gusted, carrying a sharp bite to it.

Something snapped behind her, and she spun quickly.

The small man stood there. He eyed her with a half smile.

Carth reached for the shadows and was startled to discover she could find them. The edge was there, she could pull on it, she could sink into the shadows, she could disappear within them, or—even better—she could attack using them.

She flicked her attention to the power of the flame, and it surged slightly within her.

She was no longer powerless. Whatever they had given her had worn off.

Yet she refrained. The small man didn't seem as if he were going to attack her. And she saw no reason that he snuck away. Whatever had brought him from the camp was not clear yet.

He cocked his head to the side. "You followed me." There was no surprise in his voice. It was almost as if he had expected her to follow.

"You're not with them, are you?"

The same half smile parted his mouth and he

shrugged. "With them? Perhaps for now. I let him think that he leads."

"Why? Where you going? Why are you doing this?"

"Lots of questions there. As to the first, he knows things. He has proven capable, and I think there are ways I could use him."

Use him. She heard others say the same sorts of things. What was it he intended to use the scholar for?

"Why did you sneak away?" Carth asked. "You did it the night before as well."

"You're observant. I'll give you that."

"That's no answer."

He shrugged. "Perhaps not an answer, at least not one that you would like, but that's the answer you will get."

"You're meeting someone here, aren't you?"

"Do you see anyone else? If I were meeting someone, they would be here, wouldn't they?"

Carth looked around and pulled on the shadows, drawing only the slightest amount of them, feeling a surge of relief that she could, welcoming the shadows back to her. As she did, the darkness faded, and she was able to look around her more easily.

Nothing moved in the forest at this time of night. No animals prowled in the trees. She saw a bird perched high in one of the branches, and it seemed to twist its head as if looking from her to the smaller man, before she turned her attention back to him.

He watched her, and she wondered if he knew that

she held on to the shadows. It was unlikely. Doing so would make him shadow blessed, and he did not have the look of somebody from Ih-lash.

"What now?" Carth asked.

The man was dangerous. She had seen that the first time she had seen him, noting the way he moved. Escape meant fighting him, and she could use her powers now, but she wanted to know what he was after, and why he was out here.

The man shrugged. "You could return with me. Or I could say you ran away. Either way…" He shrugged.

Carth frowned at him. "You're not going to force me back with you?"

"You should never have been captured. You were eventually going to discover how you were being contained. I'm not surprised it didn't take you very long to realize the water was not safe to drink. I'm impressed that you managed to convince him that you were still drinking the water. He's usually more observant than that."

Carth frowned. It had been a simple thing. She had dumped it out, maintaining the ruse that she actually been drinking it. "You're not going try to force me back with you?" she repeated.

The man cocked his head the other direction. "What will forcing you back accomplish? I suspect you have something else in mind, another place you intend to go."

Carth could only nod. How was it that he recognized that about her?

"Which way?" Carth asked.

"To what?"

"The wagons."

His mouth tightened. "That's what you're after. Interesting that you would think to return. Is it revenge that you seek?"

She would have her revenge, but that was secondary to the other reason she needed to return. "I'm going to see to it that no others suffer as I have."

"If you think you can rescue all of them, you're going to need to be strong and ruthless. Are you those things?"

Carth's eyes narrowed. "Ruthless? I have never been ruthless before, but after what I saw, what they were doing to the girls, I think I can manage."

"Good—"

He jerked his head around quickly.

As he did, Carth was aware of movement in the shadows. She pulled on them, sinking into them a little more than she had before, and noticed the presence of the scholar and the large man.

They must've realized she was awake, and must've realized that the smaller man had disappeared.

The large man appeared at the edge of the trees, and he eyed the smaller man.

Carth detected the scholar still back within the trees. He remained hidden.

She felt a pulsing of pressure, something that she recognized but wasn't quite sure why. It took a few moments for her to realize what that was: magic. He was using some form of magic, one that wasn't related to the A'ras magic or the shadows.

Whatever it was he used, whatever he was doing, was powerful. The air sizzled with it.

The small man shivered. He turned and spoke over his shoulder. "Go. I'll do what I can."

Carth frowned.

The scholar stepped from the trees. His eyes were wide and the hair on his head stood up slightly, as if electrified. Carth had sunk into the shadows, and she suspected that she was hidden.

"Where is she, Timothy?"

The small man shook his head. "She ran off. I chased her—"

The scholar took a step forward, power pressing away from him as he did. "You chased her?"

The large man approached well. He had a pair of curved knives now in his hand.

Carth faced a dilemma. She could escape; she had the power of the shadows and the flame burning within her, and she knew that she could get away now that she was able to reach her abilities, but... a mystery remained around this other man.

He had been willing to help her escape, even lying to the scholar. Why would he do that? Why would he have helped her, when he had seemingly been trying to help hold her captive?

The scholar took another step forward, the power pressing away from him, exploding.

Carth reacted instinctively.

She wrapped shadows around herself, extending them out toward the smaller man, creating an envelope of shadows, a bubble designed to protect them.

The explosion pressed upon her shadow bubble, squeezing her, but she pushed against it.

When the explosion passed, Carth knew that she had revealed herself.

She released the shadows, and the scholar's eyes went wide. With a nod from the scholar, the large man lumbered towards her, his large curved knives slicing as he did.

Carth jumped, pulling on the shadows, using them to power her, as she arced into the air.

As she did, she pressed out with the power of the flame, kicking with it, sending it through her foot, striking the large man in the head with power as she did. Heat and flame erupted from her foot as it collided with his head.

It felt as if she were kicking stone.

She landed in a roll.

The large man shook his head, seemingly no worse off than he had been before.

Carth pulled on the power of the flame, letting it

explode out from her. It struck the large man and dissipated.

With a sudden certainty, she understood. That was his ability. He was immune to magic, or at least immune to *her* kind of magic. He might not react to the connection she possessed to the flame, but would he be able to protect himself against the shadows?

Carth pulled on the shadows, wrapping them around her, and leapt once more, feeling the scholar using his magic at about the same time.

The area where she had just been erupted, soil and clumps of grasses flying where she had stood moments before.

While in the air, she twisted, sending the shadows down, pressing them like a blanket, trying to suffocate the big man first, wanting to know whether shadows would do anything against him.

They rolled off him.

Fighting was not an option, not unarmed as she was, not against someone who clearly had magical abilities that she did not fully understand just yet.

There was another option, one that did not involve fighting, but instead involved simply getting free. She rolled to the side, reaching for the smaller man at the same time as the scholar pulsed out with his power once more, and wrapped them in shadows, enveloping them completely.

They sank into the shadows, disappearing.

Carth took slow steps backwards, sliding with the shadows, afraid to release the connection. She would be hidden within the darkness, but she didn't know what else would happen were she to release that connection.

The smaller man glanced at her, the question on his lips reflected in his eyes.

She shook her head. They continued to step backwards. As she moved away from the larger man and the scholar, neither of them appeared to know how to follow them.

Carth continued to slide backwards, moving away from them, contained in the shadows.

When they were far enough, the smaller man—Timothy, she had heard him called—glanced back at her.

"They'll pursue us."

Carth sighed. They might pursue them, and she needed to stay ahead of the scholar and the large man. She needed to reach the wagons, reach the caravan, free the women, destroy the flat-eyed man, and reclaim her weapons.

Then, and only then, she suspected she might have a way to defeat them.

It depended upon finding Dara, reuniting with Lindy, and using those with other abilities.

"Maybe," she whispered.

They emerged onto the road, and Carth continued holding the shadows around her. "The caravan," she whispered. "Take me to the caravan, and I'll keep you safe."

The smaller man gave the same half smile and only nodded.

They traveled through the night, slowly getting farther and farther away from the other two. Carth could feel them through her connection to the shadows, and could even detect them through her connection with the A'ras flame.

She was safe, for now. She didn't know how long that would last, and hoped that it would be long enough for her to reach the wagons.

Rescue the girls. Kill the flat-eyed man. Find Dara.

She added one more: stay ahead of the scholar.

That was all she could think of.

CHAPTER 19

CARTH AND TIMOTHY HURRIED ALONG THE ROAD. THE sounds of the night enveloped her, familiarity that she had missed in the time since she had been captured. It was something she had missed without realizing it while she had been traveling by ship the last few months. There were the occasional chirping of insects, the calling of the hooting owls in the trees, the scurry of something small underfoot, and the lone howl of wolves.

The air had a crispness to it, one that carried with it the earthen odor of drying grass and the fragrance of flowers, mixed with the hints of a coming rain. For so many months, Carth had known only the smell of the sea, that of salt and fish and the stench of men long overdue for bathing. This was better.

They stopped at a stream after walking for several hours. Carth leaned in and took a few long drinks of the water, cupping it to her lips and drinking eagerly. It was clean and clear, something she had not had during her capture. As they stopped, Timothy watched her, his eyes narrowed and a wry smile turning his lips.

"When did you regain your powers?" he asked her as she took her fill of water.

It'd been so long since she had dared drinking fully, so long since she had felt anything but thirst and dry mouth. Carth let the water fill her. It rolled down her chin and she didn't bother to wipe it away. There was no need to hide the fact that she was sated.

"When you found me."

"Chathem was a fool. I still don't know why he wanted someone 'feisty.'"

"I'm more than feisty."

Timothy smiled. "I see that."

She studied him. "Where are you from?"

"Neeland." When she frowned at him, he tipped his head, the amused smile still crossing his face. "You haven't heard of Neeland?" Carth shook her head. Timothy shrugged. "I suppose that's not too uncommon. Neeland is an island to the northwest, and those who come from there are in a different industry than I suspect you are in."

"What kind of industry is that?"

"Mercenaries."

"Mercenaries? What exactly does that mean?"

Timothy patted the sword strapped to his side. "Means what I said. Most who know of Neeland know of the services they can purchase from us. That's usually the service they're after when they come looking for my people."

Carth made a point of holding on to her connection to the shadows as she had done since escaping, not knowing how much she could truly trust this man. The fact that he referred to himself as a mercenary in such casual terms made her leerier of what his intentions were.

"Why help me? If you're a mercenary, why would you go against the men who hired you?"

His smile remained, and he stood watching her with the same quizzical look in his eyes, as if he measured her, as if deciding how much to share. Since he was a mercenary, it was entirely possible that was what he did.

"I'm still on the job."

"What job is that?"

He shrugged. "Chathem wasn't my employer. I was sent to observe, look for one with particular abilities, and—"

She faded into the shadows, prepared for whatever he thought to do.

Timothy held his hands out, laughing darkly. "I'm not here to harm you. If I was here to harm you, I would've done so back in the camp when you were diminished. Now that your abilities have returned, I'm not entirely sure I *could* hurt you."

Carth released her connection, letting it fade. "Who hired you?"

Timothy kneeled by the stream, taking a long drink from the water. He glanced up at her after he did, the amused smile still on his face as it had been since they had first escaped. "I don't get a name. That's not how these things work. We're sellswords. Mercenaries. We're given a job. We do the job. We get the rest of our payment."

"So that's what I am? A job?"

Timothy stood, dusted his hands on his pants, and he shrugged. "Something like that." He nodded towards the west, the direction they were headed. Hopefully toward the wagons that Carth wanted to reach. "What's that way? Why are you after the wagons?"

Carth tipped her head at him, mimicking his smile. "You're not the only one with a job."

Timothy watched her, and after a moment he started to laugh.

They reached a narrow road late in the night. The road had evidence of recent travel: tracks were dug into the soft ground, and she saw the passing of horses, from the trampling of their hooves. She saw nothing else, nothing that would help her know whether or not the wagons had come through here or whether this was some other caravan.

Timothy studied the tracks, pacing up and down the road as he did, his eyes seeming to catch things that she didn't see. He glanced back at her after a while, his mouth pinched in a frown.

"What is it?" Carth asked.

Timothy shook his head. "I count four wagons. A dozen horses. Several men on foot." He looked up at her. "What was this? What were you expecting to find?"

Carth stared at the tracks. "Four tracks, you say?"

Timothy nodded. He motioned to the road, towards where the tracks were dug into the soft earth. "The ground is soft here, and wagons have a slightly different set to their wheels, and they don't move through identically. If you know what to look for, you can see slightly different paths moving through here, several different trails made by several different wagons. I count four. Could be I'm off, but I don't think so."

There had only been two when she was captured. Did that mean that they had met up with another? Or was it a different set of wagons?

Unfortunately, Carth suspected that they had met up with another rather than having a second set. It seemed more likely that the men traveling from Asador had met up with men traveling from one of the other great cities along the coast. If they were smuggling other women out, it made sense that they would attempt to do that from multiple places.

"These wagons carry others like me. This is where Chathem bought me."

Timothy's face darkened, his mouth tightening again, pinching into a distasteful frown. "A foul thing he thought to do. Chathem wanted to use you, though I'm not exactly sure what he intended. Most men think to use these women for other reasons."

Carth fought back the hint of anger that surged through her. "I intend to see them freed. Nothing more will happen to these women if I have anything to do with it."

"You think you're powerful enough to stop them?"

She had rarely doubted her abilities. She had faced horrible enemies in both the Hjan and the blood priests, and never had she truly felt powerless the way she had when she was captured by the slaver. Even when she was captured by Ras, she had never felt the same sort of hopelessness. He had challenged her, daring her to prove her worth, ultimately teaching her how to play the game of Tsatsun.

The man who'd captured her had wanted her for one reason, and it horrified her. It sickened her that others would be subjected to something like that. Not only her, but her friends, and those she cared about.

With resolve building in her, she nodded. "I intend to free them all, destroy the slavers, and do what I can to make sure that my friends are brought to safety."

"Good. Because we're closer then I realized." He nodded down the road.

Carth followed the direction of his nod but didn't see anything. She didn't hear anything either, but given the casual sort of competence she had seen from him, she didn't doubt that what he detected was real. On the contrary, she suspected that it was exactly what he had detected.

She reached through her connection to the shadows, wrapping them around her, fading into them, and focused on movement.

At first there was nothing, but the longer she remained concealed, wrapped within them, the more she became aware of something pressing against that power. She added a hint of the S'al magic, pulling from deep within her, letting it fill her so she could detect the heat that flickered in the distance. After a while—a dozen heartbeats, perhaps longer—she felt the steady tension from her magic, and with it she felt the distant presence of others.

Her eyes snapped open, and she turned to Timothy.

"How did you know they were there?"

He shrugged. "I'm from Neeland. We have a different sort of ability than those of your kind. Different even then those of these lands. It's sort of an awareness, one that allows us to be skilled trackers, skilled hunters. You wouldn't understand."

She studied him. She thought she *would* understand.

Holding on to the shadows, keeping herself wrapped within them, she glided down the road, moving stealthily, concealing not only herself, but also Timothy.

As they traveled, she became more and more aware of the distant sense of the others.

The caravans.

Now it was clear that Timothy had been right. There were more than two caravans. There were more than four, though, as well. She counted six, with nearly two dozen horses and nearly as many soldiers. They were camped in the night, the fire still crackling faintly. Two sentries stood guard on either end of the road.

Hidden by the shadows, she was safe, but she didn't know how long that would last. How long would they be able to maintain their safety bound by the shadows?

Carth retreated from the road and hid near a copse of trees, letting the trees provide natural coverage so that she didn't have to hold quite so tightly to the potentially unnatural shadows. Timothy watched her, his head cocked to the side almost as if listening, before turning his attention back to her.

"What did you see?"

"More than you suspected. There are six wagons and two dozen soldiers." How many more were there that she hadn't been able to count? If she played this wrong, she ran the risk not only of getting recaptured, but of losing the opportunity to get these women to freedom.

Then again, this was bigger than what she had

expected. If there were six wagons, how many more would she find if she traveled with them?

"Why are you smiling?" Timothy asked.

Carth laughed darkly. "Because I'm starting to have a different plan."

CHAPTER 20

IF CARTH WAITED TOO LONG, IT WOULD BE DAYLIGHT before she took action, and she wanted to have the safety and protection of the shadows to provide additional support. The power of the S'al would provide her increased strength, but there was safety and security in holding tightly to the shadows.

She had to play this right.

Carth thought about attacks she had been a part of in the past. There had been fights with the A'ras as well as the Reshian. With the A'ras, it had been about overwhelming whoever she faced, using the power of the flame and of the training of the A'ras. With the Reshian, they used the power of the shadows to confuse and obfuscate their presence.

There was another way, that of Ras, who used his mind to manipulate the situation into the fight he wanted. That was what she needed now.

Carth started slowly pulling on the shadows. As she did, a fog began to build, one that wasn't natural, but appeared as if it were nothing more than a simple fog.

Timothy watched her, his gaze unreadable.

Carth nodded to him. "Do you intend to observe only, or do you intend to help?" When he didn't answer her immediately, she shook her head. "I know this wasn't part of your job, and you weren't hired for this, but I saw the way you reacted when you heard me describe my time with my captors. You're no more excited about the way they use women than I am. How skilled are you with that sword?"

He laughed softly, the sound barely carrying in the fog. "You really know nothing about Neeland, do you?"

Carth shrugged. "I don't know anything about Neeland. I recognize a man with who is familiar with the sword, and likely competent. If you are, I could use you with what we're going to do here."

Timothy stood and unsheathed the sword. He made a quick few quick slashes, arcing through movements that made it clear that he had more than a passing familiarity with his sword. With a flourish, he slipped his sword back into a sheath.

"The Neelish are swordmasters. That's why we're so valued and prized as mercenaries."

Carth gazed at him a moment. She lunged, grabbing for his sword and unsheathing it, managing to do so before he could react, and recreated the same movements. When she was complete, she darted around him, flowing on the shadows, and slammed the sword back into his sheath.

"The A'ras are also swordmasters."

Timothy chuckled. "I think Chathem fully underestimated you."

Carth crossed her arms over her chest, focusing on the soldiers, the wagons, and the women inside them. "Will you help?"

Timothy nodded. "I'm not sure I have much of a choice."

"That's not an answer."

He chuckled, the sound muted in the night. "I will help."

The shadows were thick around her, held in the most potent cloak she'd ever attempted, drawn around her in a way that she had only seen once before. That was when she had traveled to Isahl and worked with Andin. She had never drawn upon the shadows herself in quite the same way, but knew that they could be used in this manner.

Draping them around her, she searched for a supply wagon first. If she could find one, come up with the right combination of medicines, she could dose the soldiers before it came to bloodshed.

It wasn't that she was opposed to fighting them, but using the shadows in the way she did gave her such an advantage that it would've felt like a slaughter. At least in this way, she felt as if she gave them a chance.

Timothy crouched next to her and leaned into her ear, whispering softly, "What will you do when they wake?"

"Most of these are simple hired help. They aren't the ones responsible for these women. When they awaken, see their women are gone, see their leaders are gone, they'll disperse and hopefully return to their homes."

"And when they don't?"

Carth clenched her jaw. "That's when they'll learn to fear me."

She paused at the first wagon, pulling the door open enough to peer inside. When she held on to the shadows in this way, it changed her perception of light, and she could see through the darkness as if it were an early-morning light.

She scanned the interior of the wagon, counting the women inside. Most were sleeping quietly, although one stared straight ahead, her gaze fixed on Carth as soon as she had opened the door. She trembled and her mouth opened as if to scream. There was no sign of Dara.

Carth brought a finger to her lips, trying to shush her before the woman did scream.

She understood this woman's fear and trepidation. She had been through enough, and likely had seen others within the wagon brought away, either to return injured or not at all.

Carth pitched her voice low. "I intend to get you to safety, but first you need to be quiet."

The woman didn't make any expression, nothing that would indicate that she understood, but she didn't scream either. Carth considered that a victory.

There were no supplies in that wagon, so she moved on to the next. Timothy followed her, his sword unsheathed, the blade barely reflecting any light. She wondered if that was something to the steel or whether it was related to the way she had him cloaked.

The inside of the next wagon was crammed with women. Some lay on the ground, side by side, packed in more tightly than in the other wagon. Several were injured, and she could smell the stink of their infection as it rotted through them. If nothing were done, the infection would likely claim them within a few days. She had seen injuries like that before, but it'd been many years, since she had traveled with her parents and her mother had performed healings. Like before, she didn't see any sign of Dara.

The fact that the slavers could let these women suffer with such injuries sickened her and steeled her resolve.

She moved to the next wagon. It was no different than the others. Already she had counted nearly a hundred women. There weren't supplies for this many women, not nearly enough food and water to keep them drugged. Unless they used the other wagons specifically for supplies. It seemed an awful waste to do that, especially as space seem to be at a premium, but it was just the sort of heartless things she would expect from the slavers, especially knowing that what they intended to do with these women.

Where was Dara?

Had she *not* been brought out of the city this way?

The next wagon held mostly food and a few casks of water. One smelled of wine, and the red stain on the wood confirmed it. She doubted the women ever saw the wine and suspected they saw little of the food either.

The next wagon was different.

Two bunks were set on either side of the walls. Men rested on them. One snored, taking deep, sonorous breaths. Carth held on to the shadows, drawing away even more of the night so that she could study these men.

There was the flat-eyed man.

Her heart quickened.

Here was the man who'd captured her. He'd poisoned her. All she wanted was revenge.

But… if she obtained revenge now, she would miss the chance to understand what exactly they were doing with these women. She needed to know where they headed with them. Wasn't that the point of the lessons she had learned from her Tsatsun master? She needed patience, and needed to be able to arrange her pieces so that when she did act, there could be only one move-ment—the one that she wanted.

The movement she wanted was the one that provided her with answers as to who these men worked for, and where they brought the women.

There had been a time when she'd been willing to use others in a greater move, but after what she'd been through, she couldn't leave these women here.

She slipped into the wagon, padding across the floor on feet muted by her magical abilities. She searched for how they'd sedated the women. It was the same way she would see them sedated.

A trunk pushed up against the far wall caught her attention. Carth cracked the lid, and inside she saw three large jars filled with a familiar white powder. It was a same powder Chathem had intended to use upon her.

Carth grabbed all three jars and backed out of the wagon, retreating from the men.

Timothy waited for her outside, his sword unsheathed.

"Is this it?" She held up the contents of the trunk.

Timothy pried open the top of one of the canisters. He dipped his head close and took a deep breath. "This is slithca. This will be enough to sedate. If any of them have any extra abilities, this will prevent them from reaching them."

"That's a foul sort of powder," Carth said.

Timothy chuckled, and Carth made a point of

keeping the sound muted. "The powder is far better than what most in these lands know. They know it as a syrup, and the syrup is particularly awful."

"How can I dose them with this?"

"A little of the powder placed in their mouth or beneath their nose so that they inhale it will do the trick. It will achieve the same goal as if you had forced them to drink it, or even injected it. The concentrated nature makes it even more potent. Something like that will probably last for several days. By the time they awaken, we should be far from here."

"Why didn't Chathem use the powder on me that way?"

Timothy chuckled again. "Chathem didn't dare use it on you in that concentrated a form. He didn't know what abilities you possessed, and he didn't know how long he would need to suppress them, and he only had a single vial. Had he used too much, he risked you regaining your abilities before you were able to be brought to the end destination."

Carth frowned. "You're saying I'm lucky?"

"Not lucky. Just that he was conservative. He had calculated the likelihood of your escape, balancing that versus his need for ongoing suppression and knowing that in liquid form he could continue to dose you in such a way that you would be suppressed indefinitely. I think he played the odds."

"It was a game he lost," Carth said.

Timothy eyed her a moment, and then nodded.

Carth took the canister and kept herself wrapped in the shadows. She held on to an edge of the A'ras magic and slipped back inside the wagon. She took a pinch of powder and dropped it into each man's mouth, catching it as they breathed.

The man snoring presented a difficult challenge. When he blew out, he puffed the powder towards her. Carth had a moment of fear that she would lose her ability with the shadows, that she would lose that suppression, but wrapped in the shadows and with the flame magic, the powder seemed to burn off in the air and a burst of sparks. She dosed him a second time, just to be safe.

She moved out of the wagon and began making her way through the camp. Most of the soldiers were sleeping, making it easy for her to dose them with the powder. The two sentries were a little more difficult. Timothy helped with that, sneaking up behind them and striking them on the back of the head with his sword so that Carth could then dose them with her powder.

"Is that everyone?" Timothy asked.

Carth focused on the power of the S'al magic, using that to detect flickers of heat, and when that didn't give her a clear answer, she shifted to listening with the power of the shadows. She didn't detect anything that would indicate others that she might've missed.

"I think so."

Timothy nodded to the line of horses. "We should

take all of them. They move faster, and we'll be able to keep them from catching us."

Together they began hitching the horses to the wagons. When they were done, Carth hesitated. She glanced back to the wagon where the men had been bunked, and her gaze skipped to the remaining wagon that she hadn't yet investigated. What if they had missed one with women in it?

"Where you going?" Timothy asked.

"I need to check on that one."

She waved down the road, motioning towards Timothy. "Get the wagons moving, and get the women out of here. I will catch you soon as this is done."

Timothy nodded and started the horses, shaking reins to get them walking, motioning them forward.

When the wagons had cleared the area, leaving the sedated soldiers as well as the remaining three wagons, Carth hurried into the one she hadn't yet investigated.

Inside, she found weapons of all sorts. Several of them reminded her of the one that had punctured her hand and left her injured. That was not the kind of weapon she wanted to leave.

Where were her knives?

Carth searched the collection along the walls before moving on to the drawers. Inside one of the drawers she came across her shadow knife. She found her A'ras knife as well and slipped both into her waistband.

Leaving the wagon, on a whim, she sent a surge of power of the A'ras flame through the wood of the wagon, heating it to an extreme temperature, and it began burning red hot.

At least they wouldn't be able to use the weapons.

As Carth slipped down the road, into the night and after the wagons, she felt a hint of hope.

CHAPTER 21

THEY TRAVELED THROUGH THE NIGHT, GUIDING THE horses along the road until they met an intersecting road that was harder-packed than the one they had been traveling. Timothy had shown himself to be quite skilled at guiding the horses, leading them rapidly so that Carth had to race to keep up. She had little experience with horses, much like she had once had little experience with sailing, but she saw the way Timothy steered them and noted the way he prompted them with simple commands.

Carth mimicked him, trying to learn the commands. There would come a time when she would need to help with the wagons, and she wanted to be ready. They hadn't attempted to free the women, not wanting to frighten them so that the women panicked and made it more difficult for them to get them to freedom, but she would need to let them know soon.

As light gradually swept across the sky, the sun rising in beautiful streaks of color, fatigue began to overwhelm her.

How long had she been away? The attack had taken much out of her, as had the escape. Then there had been the race to get to the wagons, all of which had required that she use her magical abilities, something she had not done in several days, possibly even weeks. She was no longer certain how long she had been gone from Asador.

When she began to stumble, Timothy signaled to her that they should halt. "We don't have to keep pushing like this."

Carth shook her head. "We have to keep moving. We don't want them to catch us."

It wasn't all she was concerned about. She didn't have supplies for the women, nothing to provide them with food or water, and the longer they traveled, the more likely it was they would starve.

Moving quickly would allow her to get them to a place where they could get some help that much sooner, but she still didn't know quite where they were heading. Timothy had taken them east, back in the same direction Carth had first traveled.

She thought about her options. Asador would have places where she could find help, but it required that she find others willing to risk themselves. Would they be able to keep these women safe? That was her biggest concern at this point. She wasn't willing to have rescued them only to turn around and lose them once more to the same people who'd captured them the last time.

"I'm not sure where to take them to get them to safety."

"There are a few places, but you said there were nearly a hundred women?" When Carth nodded, he let out a slow sigh. "That's a lot of people to try to hide. We need a bigger city, or someplace where they wouldn't think to look in the first place."

And it had to happen fast. Carth needed the wagons to finish what she intended. She wanted to draw the attackers away, and wanted to entice them into thinking that they could recover the women.

She thought she could follow them and use that to discover more about their operation. If she could, then she could ensure this didn't happen again.

"There's a village not far from here," Timothy began. "It's not a large place, but I've had some dealings with them and know them to be fiercely independent. They have no interest in trading like this. They might be able to help."

"What village is that?"

"It's a coastal village. Goes by the name of Praxis."

Carth scratched her chin. Coastal meant she could reach it by ship. Once she found Dara and Guya, they would be able to check on the women.

"How far?"

"From here? Probably only a few hours more. We can reach it before morning for certain."

Carth took a deep breath and realized she didn't have much choice. Not if she intended to trap the slavers, and not if she intended to find out more about their operation.

They reached the village of Praxis well after midnight. It was dark, and the sounds of the sea crashing on rocks was a familiar one to her, one that reminded her of Nyaesh and all the cities she had traveled in the time since she had left. Despite enjoying the scents of the forest, and those of the grasses and flowers, there was a familiarity to the sea, one that she had somehow grown comfortable with.

They brought the wagons in to the edge of town. Timothy motioned to her, and Carth waited at his suggestion, not certain what he intended at this point. They had spoken little since deciding to make their way to Praxis. Carth was fine with that, especially as she was barely able to keep her eyes open on the walk. She found herself pulling on the shadows, using that to provide the energy she needed to keep going. Despite that, she still struggled to maintain a steady pace. She was happy when they reached the village.

While Timothy was heading into the village, Carth decided it was time to search through the wagons more closely, looking for Dara. That was the reason she had disappeared in the first place, and the reason she had risked so much.

Would she even find her friend?

The first wagon she opened had fewer women in it than the others. She pressed through the S'al magic, letting a soft glow light her hand, and surveyed the faces within. Dara was not here. She recognized several of the other women, having seen them when she had been a captive. They needed food, and safety, but she didn't dare do anything until they were within Praxis.

At the next wagon, she pulled open the door to see the crowd of women. They all looked at her with an expectant expression. Many of them cast their gaze to the ground, afraid. Carth had seen that same expression from too many people over the years. Had she worn it herself? She no longer knew. She held aloft the light, searching for her friend, but saw no sign of her there either.

That left the third wagon. She didn't recall seeing her when she had searched through them the night before, but then, Carth's goal had been simply to help rescue the wagons, and to secure all that she could.

She pulled open the door, looked inside, and searched for Dara. With the light glowing from her palm, she scanned the faces. Many were covered in dirt and grime, and there were women with different colors of hair, different colors of skin, and women of all different ages. None of which were Dara.

Carth took a step back. Fatigue continued to overwhelm her. She pulled on the shadows, reaching through them with all the strength she could. Unintentionally, she sank into them, retreating, but there was no nothing else she could do. She closed the door of the wagon and sank to her knees.

All of this had been started to find her friend, and she had failed.

Tears streamed down her face. It took a moment to for her to realize and understand why she was so upset. She recognized that it was more than the fact that Dara was missing. It was knowing the likely reason why she was missing. If Dara was not here, she likely had already been sold.

She was tired.

So tired.

She needed rest.

Without meaning to, she sank to the ground, and sleep overcame her.

CHAPTER 22

A HAND ON HER SHOULDER WOKE CARTH FROM A DEEP slumber. She had dreamed, but the dreams made little sense. There had been nothing in them other than visions of men with dangerous weapons. She had flashes of her past, flashes of her parents, even, but for the most part it was a dreamless sleep.

Timothy looked down at her, his half smile still crossing his face, this time mixed with something that resembled concern.

"You extended yourself too far."

Carth sat up and glanced around a small room. It was simple and plain, with walls of wood and a curtain covering the window. She was on a flat mattress, with sheets more comfortable than anything she'd slept on in weeks. A bowl of water rested on a stand next to her. An unlit lantern was next to the water. And Timothy, sitting on the edge of the bed, his hands clasped in his lap.

"What choice did I have but to extend myself?"

Timothy flashed a smile. "Perhaps none. You will be pleased to know that the village council has agreed to support the women. They will be safe. At least for now."

Carth breathed out a sigh. It was a relief knowing the women would be safe. She wasn't sure how long such safety would last, not with slavers who had access to soldiers and weapons and poisons, tactics that would enable them to search for the women in a way that didn't necessarily keep them safe indefinitely. This was a temporary safety, but now that she was awake, Carth was more determined than ever to ensure that it became a permanent safety. She would see that slavers were not able to torment these women any longer. If she would be able to give them anything, that was the gift she could offer.

"Where are they?"

"Praxis is a village of nearly five hundred. Everyone has been willing to take in several of the women. They're getting food, water, and a place to stay."

Carth stood and reached for the shadows and then the flame. She tested her connection, the time when she had lost it making her fearful of that time returning. Both responded, though Carth hadn't expected that they wouldn't. Timothy had helped her, and she was not surprised to note that he made no threatening movement towards her now that they were there.

"What do you intend to do?" Timothy asked.

"I still intend to complete my plan."

Timothy studied her, his eyes nearly as intense as Chathem's had been when he'd studied her, as if he knew things that he shouldn't necessarily know. It was possible that he did, and possible that he had determined something about her in the time they had traveled together. Carth didn't know if he had, and wasn't entirely sure that she cared.

"The person I was trying to find wasn't in the wagons."

"This was all about finding one person?"

"It started that way. And now that I haven't found her, this isn't over." She looked to Timothy, knowing that there would be value if he were to stay and protect the women, but there would be just as much value if he were willing to come with her, especially with what she intended. She needed help.

Carth thought about others who had helped her in the past, about Lindy and Guya and all the shadow blessed. She wished she had their support right now.

"What of you? You still have a job to do?"

Timothy shrugged. "There is a job. It will get done."

"I need to get back to the wagons and lead them away from Praxis so that they don't realize what we were doing. That's the other part of what I planned. I want to use them—"

"About that…"

"What you mean?"

"Well, there is a price to letting the women remain within the village. There was a cost to providing supplies and safety and food and shelter."

It was more than all of that. Praxis offered hope. "You gave them the wagons?"

"Not the wagons. They have no interest in that. But the horses…"

"What of the wagons, then?" Carth asked. She had stopped at the door leading out from the small room. Light leaked in around the edge of the door, enough that it was well into the daytime. How long had she been sleeping?

Long enough for her to feel refreshed. Long enough for her no longer to feel as if she were about to fall over. She considered questioning the women, searching for answers about where Dara might have gone, but none of them would've known. They feared for their safety and would have been trapped in the wagons. They wouldn't have known anything about what had happened to the women taken from the wagons in the middle of the night.

Had Dara ever been one of the women in the wagons? Carth hadn't seen her when she was captured, only knowing what the flat-eyed man had said. He had suggested that Dara had been captured, but then had also suggested that she had been taken to another man —Terran.

It all came back to the same answer. She needed to discover what they intended, and find the slavers.

"The wagons were sent over the cliff edge, and they crashed into the sea." Timothy wore a look of grim satisfaction as he shared that with her. "In time, the froth in the sea will grind the remains of the wagons into little more than debris."

Carth allowed herself to smile at the thought. That would be a fitting outcome for the wagons. "Good."

She pulled open the door and stepped into the village. She was in a small house at the edge of the village. Several men led horses through it. They talked animatedly to each other, occasionally slapping the side of the horse to guide it. Others carried baskets, or barrels, all moving with a sort of determination and purpose.

When this was over, when she had determined more about the man who thought to harm women like this, she would return. There was something she could offer, but not yet. And perhaps not all of these women would be willing to help. She would offer it to those who were.

She headed out of the village. Timothy followed, saying nothing. Carth checked to ensure her knives were still with her, though she should've done it before even leaving the small room, and was not surprised to find that they still were strapped to her side.

Timothy noted the gesture. "I've seen weapons like that before."

There was a hint of something more in the comment, though she couldn't tell if it was accusation or something else.

Carth tapped the knife she'd claimed after her mother had died, the one that she had for so long thought was an A'ras blade; now she understood it was a blade from Ih-lash, possibly even one her father had made. "This one is for the shadows." She tapped the other knife, the one she had helped to craft that gave her a greater connection to her S'al magic. "And this one is for the flame."

Timothy only nodded.

After they had walked for a while, Timothy spoke up. "Do you intend to share your plan with me?"

Carth shrugged. "I intend to follow them. I'm going to find their network."

Timothy chuckled. "Their network? Do you think to rescue all the women they capture?"

Carth looked over at him, a hard expression in her eyes. Timothy met it, not shrinking away. "I intend to find their network and destroy it."

CHAPTER 23

CARTH REACHED THE TRAIL OF THE SLAVERS LATE THAT night.

They traveled by foot, making their way off the road, weaving through long grasses. Timothy found the path; he had a knack for following trails and noting where others might be, with his special ability with tracking.

The trail led through the grasses, and they moved slowly, pausing every so often as they did, investigating places where it seemed as if they had branched off and taken a different pathway. For the most part, the slavers seemed to travel across the ground.

"How many do you think there are?" Carth asked Timothy after they had trailed them for nearly an hour.

"This is only about a half dozen."

Carth turned back and looked at him sharply.

"What of the rest? What happened to all the soldiers we sedated?"

"I don't see evidence of the soldiers. There are few men moving through here, and they seem to have a destination in mind. Otherwise they wouldn't move across ground like this. Besides, I suspected you wanted to follow these men rather than the dozen soldiers that traveled along the road."

"Are they traveling to Praxis?"

Timothy shook his head. "Not to Praxis. I made certain there would be no way to follow that path."

"How did you manage that?"

"Is that something you really think you need to know?"

Carth considered pressing him. It would be helpful to know what he had done, just as it would be helpful to know whether she really could trust him. He was a mercenary. He made no qualms about that fact, just as he had made it clear that he still had a job to complete. Would that job would put them into opposition before this was over, or would helping her ultimately help him?

For now, she decided it didn't matter.

"You left the soldiers traveling on the road?"

"You were the one who didn't feel they needed to be removed from the game."

From the game? That seemed a comment she would've made. She began watching Timothy with a different interest, worried that perhaps she had misread his moves.

She thought back to what he had done in the time since she'd met him. He'd only helped her once she had followed him into the woods, but had he intended for her to follow him?

It was possible that he had.

They continued following the trail through the grasses. As they went, it became even clearer that they followed the right path. She saw evidence of several individual footprints, though she wasn't quite sure whether these were soldiers or the slavers she'd dosed in the wagon.

At one point, Timothy paused near a small pond. Carth closed her eyes and let herself use the combination of the shadows and the flame, searching for any sort of connection she might be able to detect, and noted the very clear and distinct sense of several individuals who had passed through here.

What was more, she had a sense of something else.

Was it magical ability? She had thought that the powder she'd used on them would've suppressed anything they could have done, but it was possible that the powder hadn't been effective. It was also possible that Timothy had not been completely honest with her about the effects of the powder. It certainly seemed to sedate the men, but what if he had misled her about what else it could do?

"You're looking at me strangely," Timothy said.

Carth only shrugged. "I think I have to consider all possibilities."

Timothy chuckled. "You wouldn't be worth what price they put on you if you didn't."

"What price is that?"

Timothy nodded to the water, pausing there before continuing. "What do you see there?" he asked, pointing to two indentations near the shore of the pond.

Carth suppressed an amused smile. He was avoiding answering, and what was more, he seemed to want her to know that he avoided answering.

What game did he play at?

It was possible that he knew how to play the game Tsatsun much like she did, but she got the sense that he was playing a different game. It was one she needed to understand so that she could know her role in the game, but perhaps it was one that she could position within the game she had to play.

"I see nothing."

"Hmm. Perhaps it's nothing."

They continued away from the pond, weaving through the grasses. Day turned into night, and shadows stretched across the land, growing thicker. Carth didn't even need to pull on them to fully sink into them. They were there, and she felt them, but she didn't draw upon their strength.

There was no need. She remained connected to them, holding on to that connection, not wanting to lose it, but more than that, she wanted to have the strength of the shadows if she needed it. Along with it, she held a trickle of the flame. She had grown more skilled at maintaining this connection, something that once would have been incredibly difficult for her.

Now she was able to hold on to it and preserve that connection, use it so that she wouldn't be surprised and have to reach for it suddenly. Perhaps that was why she had grown weakened so quickly when rescuing the women from the wagons. Holding on to the flame, much more so than using the shadows, taxed her strength.

They passed through the grassy plains and onto an open field near midnight. The moon hung high overhead, thick and full, glowing with a soft yellowish light that sent silver streaks across the land. The occasional howl of a wolf seemed to startle Timothy, but it never startled Carth.

As she moved through the plains, heading towards a dark smear of forest, she detected the presence of shadows upon her. It was a steady sense, one that seem to push against her shadows, one that alerted her to others.

She paused, surveying the forest in the distance.

"Yes, that is the same forest," Timothy said.

Why would the slavers have headed for the same forest she had escaped from?

What had she missed?

"Tell me what I'm missing, Timothy. Who is Chathem?"

The amused smile spread across his face. "Now she begins to ask the right questions."

CHAPTER 24

THEY HAD NEARLY MOVED THROUGH THE FOREST BY THE time Carth caught sight of the slavers. They were camped, a small fire set up in the middle of a clearing crackling softly against the night. A thin trail of smoke filtered up to the treetops. One man stood watch, looking out over the rest of them.

Carth saw no sign of Chathem or the large man. It was too coincidental for the slavers to be here, and she knew that he must be here as well.

Timothy hadn't known much more than Carth did about Chathem. He knew that he was skilled and recognized that he must have some other abilities, but he hadn't learned anything more than that.

Carth questioned whether Timothy had been hired to come after the scholar, but the sellsword was noncommittal about that. That didn't trouble her nearly so much as trying to understand what else she might've missed.

She'd thought she had been observant. What if she had missed her opportunity to eliminate one of the bigger threats? Chathem could ignore her abilities, and the large man had seemed immune to her powers. There had to be something about them that she could learn.

Timothy remained hidden, keeping away from her as they scouted so that more than one of them might be able to react if someone crept upon them.

Carth sat and watched.

There was nothing else she could do, nothing else that she really *needed* to do. This was the reason she'd allowed the slavers to live. She needed information and wanted to know what they intended and where they would go.

She sat motionless, shrouded by shadows. At least she couldn't be detected this way.

Night passed slowly, giving her time to consider what else she needed to do.

Once she discovered the leader of the slavers—a man whose name she had heard but whom she had never met—she needed to find what they might have done with Dara. She had no doubt they were connected, but why had they claimed her?

And was there any connection to Guya? Had they harmed him to get to Dara or to Carth?

Dara would have been poisoned at some point, but Carth still didn't understand how or why her friend had been chosen. What was it about her friend that made them want her? Dara had Lashasn ability, much like Carth did, but it didn't seem to her like that ability had been targeted. More than that, her ability should've protected Dara.

Maybe they hadn't recognized Dara's flame ability. If that was the case, then there was another reason, something she didn't understand.

Or it could simply be the fact that Dara was a beautiful woman. If that was what the slavers were after, she understood why they would target Dara.

Carth hated the fact that she had been unable to protect her friend, and that she had failed her. With all her abilities, with all her power, she hadn't been able to protect her friend. For that matter, Carth had barely been able to protect herself.

As the night passed and slowly turned into day, Carth remained motionless, holding on to the shadows and drawing strength from them, using that to help her stay alert. There was no movement, nothing other than the changing of the sentry.

As daylight bloomed in the sky overhead, the flat-eyed man awoke and turned his attention to the others.

Carth clenched her shadow knife. Anger seethed through her at seeing him awake. She should have killed him. He had a slight lethargy to him that he hadn't had before, and she wondered if perhaps she had overlooked some magical ability that he possessed.

It was possible that he was powered in some way. Had that been how he had captured her? She had been poisoned, but there was such an easy way about how he had managed to do it that she believed that maybe there was something more, something she hadn't fully understood.

"When do you expect them?"

This came from the man who had been sentry when they had first appeared in the forest. He had slept, snoring softly as he did, until morning, when they all had awoken.

"We were told to return here if there were any issues. If they're not here, we just have to keep moving and reach the city."

Carth sat back.

They intended to travel onward to a city. What were the odds that they might go to Asador? Could she follow them all the way there?

The men broke camp and started off through the forest. Timothy watched from the opposite side of the clearing. He seemed to see through her concealment, as if he could part the shadows.

What ability did he possess? Tracking—that much she knew—but it was more than that.

She nodded to him and they started off, following the flat-eyed man and the slavers away from the trees.

By evening, Carth knew that they were making their way towards Asador. The city spread with bright lights on the horizon, and she smelled the salt in the air once more. It was a welcoming odor, one that could bring her to safety. All she had to do was return to the ship, if the *Goth Spald* remained in port.

But did it? After all the time she'd been away, what if someone else had taken possession of the ship? Lindy might've remained in the city, but Guya had gone missing at the same time as Dara.

"You've been quiet."

Carth glanced over to Timothy. "There isn't anything to say. They return to Asador. You know this is where I came from?"

"I think you came from somewhere else. Asador might've been where you were captured, and where they brought you away from, but your origin… that is something else."

Carth smiled. She had thought the scholar the observant one, but Timothy had proven equally observant.

"From somewhere else. But now I think I will stay here."

Timothy's brow furrowed as he stared at her. "These lands are unfamiliar to you. What would make you want to remain here?"

For Carth, it was about more than simply what she'd seen taking place in these lands. There was danger here. The women were treated poorly, and the others she had seen in the city had been frightened.

And then there was the underlying concern she had for the Hjan. These lands were home to them, and more than anything else, she needed to keep an eye on them. Wasn't that the reason she had come across the sea in the first place?

There was still something about the Hjan that she didn't fully understand. When she did, she would have to decide whether she helped maintain the peace, continuing with the Accords that she had agreed to, or whether she would push against them and destroy the Hjan.

Carth didn't answer, and they continued trailing after the soldiers, following them into the city as the men tried to blend into the crowds, moving quietly through the throng of people. Carth noted children scurrying through the streets, hands occasionally drifting into pockets, collecting scraps as she had once done. Once again, she smiled as she saw this. Children like that could move unnoticed. Much in the same way that the women in the taverns had gone unnoticed until the slavers grabbed them.

"Why are you grinning?" Timothy asked as they continued weaving through the streets.

As the slavers slowed, Carth caught sight of a yellow door. She had seen it before.

It couldn't be coincidental that these men would

travel to the same yellow door. It had been where she had brought Dara.

"Only an idea," Carth said. It was one that would take some time to develop, but the more she thought about it, the more she began to wonder if it had merit.

First, she needed to complete this task. She would finish dealing with these slavers; only then would she be able to begin dealing with other issues.

Carth lingered, watching the men as they reached the yellow door. One by one, they entered.

"What is it?"

Carth shook her head. Why this healer? Had Guya known?

He wouldn't have betrayed them this way. Guya was their friend. They had been through so much together that she knew better than to think that Guya would betray them.

More than that, Guya had hated the idea of women taken by slavers. She had seen that from the very beginning. That was how she had known she could trust him.

No... she needed to shake those thoughts from her mind. She tried arranging the pieces that she recognized in her mind, but couldn't come up with an answer. All moves she did come up with were troubling.

There had to be a different answer. She just had to figure out what it was.

CHAPTER 25

CARTH CROUCHED IN FRONT OF THE WINDOW OF THE healer's shop. She saw movement behind the window, but it was mostly shadows. The night air had a crispness to it, and she wished for a warmer cloak, but was thankful that she had any coverage.

Nothing else moved along the street. They were alone here, standing in front of the door as they waited. How long did she risk waiting?

They would have to go in soon if she was to discover what had happened, and why the slavers had come here. It *could* be chance, but it didn't feel like it.

Why this shop? Why would the slavers have come here of all places? It had been empty when she'd last been here, abandoned after what had seemed like an attack.

She glanced over to Timothy, but he said nothing,

leaning casually against the wall of the building, looking almost as if he simply waited for someone.

She ducked low and remained beneath the window, trying to listen. An occasional sound drifted out, including something that sounded like a whimper, but she wasn't certain whether it was real or not.

She needed to get inside the shop.

When she had been here before and found it empty, she hadn't explored enough to know whether there was a rear entrance. Then again, when she had first come, the older healer had disappeared out the back. There *had* to be another entrance.

She nodded to Timothy and hurried around the side of the building before turning down one of the side streets. He said nothing, trailing willingly and not seeming concerned about the fact that Carth hadn't explained what they were doing.

They came upon an alley, and she turned down it. The alley was narrow, barely wide enough for the two of them to walk side by side. Doors from buildings on either side of them lined the alley, with most locked.

She paused about midway down the alley. How far had she gone? Which one of these doors would belong to the healer's shop?

"That one." Timothy pointed towards a door that had once been painted a dark brown but now had faded and chipped overtime. The handle gleamed with a soft silver.

Carth grabbed the handle and found it locked. Likely it was barred from the other side as well. "How sure are you that this is it?"

He looked over at her, a bemused expression on his face. "How certain? I think I've proven my tracking ability, haven't I?" As Carth tried the handle again, Timothy chuckled. "I'd think your abilities would come in handy here."

Carth gripped the handle, pressing heat through her palm, sending it slowly oozing through the door. With that connection, she felt the metal shifting.

An inspiration came to her.

She pressed through the door, triggering it with the shadows. It was almost as if the shadows knew what was asked of them. The lock clicked softly, and the door started to open before meeting resistance.

Barred. She had suspected that it would be, and finding that it was didn't surprise her.

She wanted to get in quietly. Doing anything else, triggering it in any other way, ran the risk of exposing her to those inside. Somehow, she needed to lift the barricade without getting discovered.

She needed to find out what exactly was blocking the door. Pressing heat through the doorway, she used that to trace the contours of the bar, letting it tell her the shape and nature of the obstruction.

Could she lift the bar?

Not with her hands, but maybe with the shadows if

she were to use them in such a way that she thickened them, made them something more corporeal.

Carth began twisting the shadows, thickening them so that she could pull up on the bar. She had never attempted anything quite like this before, but she had known that she could use the shadows in ways that she had not fully explored. They were for more than to cloak her, and more than to strengthen herself. There had been times when she had wished for someone to teach her, another shadow born or even a skilled shadow blessed, but she had fumbled along on her own, managing well enough. She would do so now.

The bar lifted free.

Carth held it in place, not wanting to drop it and make noise. She held on to it, but she didn't dare move. If she did, she feared she'd lose the connection to the shadows, and lose the connection to the barricade.

"I need you to go in and grab this before it falls."

Timothy studied her for a moment and then nodded.

He slipped past her, pushing the door open barely enough to slide inside, and then she felt him lift the bar from her shadow grasp.

Letting out a relieved sigh, Carth released the connection to the shadows and joined him inside the healer's shop.

The back side of the shop was quite a bit different than the front. There was a row of low shelves, all cluttered with different leaves and berries, but these were not labeled. Carth suspected that many of these were more dangerous than the ones on the other side of the shop.

Two doors led off from here. One she recognized as leading into the shop itself. The other most likely led into a side building.

The door off to the side compelled her. Carth tried the handle and found it locked.

Why would this door be locked?

"Watch that door," Carth told Timothy. "Listen and see if you can hear anything useful. And keep anyone from coming through it."

Timothy smiled at the command but nodded his agreement.

Carth steadily began building energy through the lock, thickening it the same way she had the last time with the shadows, grasping the locking mechanism in some way that she didn't fully understand. It clicked, and the door unlocked.

Unlike the outer door, there was no other barricade. The door came open, revealing a darkened room on the other side. A foul odor met her nose. It was the stink of sickness, that of vomit and rot.

Rather than pulling on the shadows to retreat into the darkness, she used the power of the flame and pressed it through her palm as she had done when looking into the wagons. Light bloomed in her hand and she could look around.

Her stomach dropped.

Rows of benches occupied this room. On each bench sat nearly two dozen different women. Some were children, barely more than ten or eleven.

All the women appeared to be drugged in some way. None of them reacted as she entered. None moved, barely looking up when she opened the door.

Could the healer be complicit in finding women for the slavers?

She recognized one of the women. It was a girl from the tavern, a woman Julie had worried about getting abducted.

There was another door on opposite side of the room. Before rescuing these women, she needed to know what was taking place. She paused at that door, noting that, like the other, it was locked. She unlocked it the same as she had the other two.

This room was different than the others, and well-lit by lanterns stationed around the room. It was ornately decorated, with a gilded desk that filled much of the middle of the room.

A man sat at the desk and looked up as soon as she entered.

Carth wrapped him in heat and shadows as she darted towards him. The shadows muffled his shout. The heat was intended as a mild torment.

She stabbed him in the shoulder with her knife, pressing shadows through it, which began creeping along his arms. He screamed again, but she continued to muffle him with her connection to the shadows.

"We're going to talk, you and I."

The man's eyes widened. She eased the muffling back enough to allow him to speak, though she was prepared to stuff it back down his throat, using the shadows as a gag if she needed to.

"Who... who are you?"

Carth shook her head. "I'm the one who gets to ask the questions."

The man licked his lips and swallowed. His head swiveled, eyes darting around the room, but Carth had maintained her draw on the shadows, forcing his attention back to her.

"Who's in charge here?"

Carth felt a sudden pressure against the shadows. She had recognized it before, had felt it when she was traveling into the city. It was a surge of power that diminished her shadows.

It didn't eliminate them altogether—she was wrapped too tightly in them for that, and she held on to the power of the flame as well, which prevented her from losing her connection altogether—but... her shadows faded.

A door on the opposite side of the room opened. The man she knew as Chathem, the scholar who had purchased her and carried her through the forest, stood opposite her. A dark smile twisted his mouth.

"Ms. Rel, I believe? Interesting that you should return here. I think I will enjoy discovering why." He started towards her, a pair of knives appearing in his hands.

Carth blinked slowly, drawing upon the strength of the shadows and the strength of the flame as she unsheathed her knives. "As will I."

CHAPTER 26

CARTH APPROACHED THE MAN SLOWLY, KNIVES CLUTCHED in her hands. She kept herself wrapped in the shadows, pulling upon them and trying to retreat into them, but something he did pushed against them. It was as if he had some way of countering her use of them.

She fought, pulling on the shadows in a way that allowed her to hold on to them, clutching them, afraid that he might be able to do something that would prevent her from maintaining that connection. What he did this time was not like the poisoning, when she couldn't reach either shadow or flame. This was a magical resistance.

Carth mixed her two magical powers together. They surged within her, a flash of power that filled her with her combined energies.

She poured them out through her knives as she attacked.

The man was quick. He managed to catch her first attack and turned it away.

Carth lunged, slicing towards him, sweeping her knives around, dropping to the ground as she did.

He backed away, holding his knives in front of him. The air seemed to ripple in front of him. Pressure built away from him, taking Carth's breath away. If she didn't act now, she suspected he would continue to drive her backwards.

Her feet slipped upon the ground, and there was nothing she could do.

The man smiled at her, the malevolent grin he'd worn when he'd first captured her returning to his face. "You really would've been quite the intriguing study."

With that, she shifted her focus, pushing with her power of flame into the ground, anchoring herself. It held her in place, and with a surge of heat and fire, she jumped towards him.

"Why does everybody keep thinking that I'm something to study?"

She slashed at him, catching him in the chest with the knife powered by her S'al magic.

He staggered back, and blood poured from where her knife had connected.

She twisted, trying to reach him with her shadow knife. This one missed, and he caught her wrist, bending it down.

Carth tried swinging with her free hand, wanting to

catch him with the knife summoning the flame, but he held on with an iron grip.

Her arm snapped.

Carth screamed. Pain raced through her body, a terrible, burning sensation, and she lost her grip on the knife. The pain severed her connection to both the shadows and the flame. She was unable to think of anything but pain.

Carth scrambled back, trying to get away, but he held on to her useless arm.

"I think I'll be a little more careful with your dosing this time. Once we reach Fylan, you will be less trouble for me. From there, I will take my time studying you. I think your abilities will provide much insight."

Carth hadn't heard of Fylan but didn't think she would be able to escape him again if she were captured. Escaping once had been luck, mixed with a little skill. A second escape would be less likely, especially now that he knew she had managed to escape once. He would watch her closely, and she feared the way he would use her.

She swung her good arm around, twisting with the knife, but he squeezed on the broken arm. Carth nearly dropped her other knife, and it was only by chance that she did not.

He dragged her towards the door. If he brought her where the other women were, if he chained her and dosed her with whatever poison he used to confine the others, she would not be able to escape.

She kicked, driving the heel of her boot towards him, but the man jumped, carrying her with her.

Her arm throbbed as he did, pain racing through her arm, jolting up it like a thousand needles stabbing into her skin. It was something like when she'd first begun summoning the power of the flame. At that time, she'd experienced it as a burning sensation within her blood, a fire that tore through her when she tried pulling on that magic.

This was a hundred times worse.

If she didn't do anything, she would be dragged into the other room. Carth blocked the pain out, forcing it away from her thoughts, trying to create nothing but a blank slate within her mind.

It was difficult, the overwhelming pain searing through her making it hard to think of anything else, but she needed to overcome this.

They reached the door. The scholar's hand touched the doorknob.

Carth closed her eyes. She was not helpless, and he had not defeated her—not yet. She could still reach the shadows, and she could still reach the flame, though the connection was difficult with the pain searing through her.

She could use the magic to suppress the pain, possibly even to heal herself. All she had to do was reach them.

The connection was difficult, but it was not impossible. She had suffered pain before, and she had survived it. That was what she was: a survivor. She had power, she had magic, but she had survived things that should have killed her time and again.

This man—this *scholar*—would not claim her.

Carth breathed out.

As she did, the shadows and the flame mixed together, creating something much like what Ras had used when he had first attacked her. It exploded from her, and the scholar staggered back, losing his grip on her arm.

Carth clutched the broken arm against her. It hurt less than she had expected. She sent power spilling through the broken arm, stabilizing it with magic much as her mother had once stabilized others with her herbs.

The pain receded enough that she could function.

Anger surged through her. This was the man who had attempted to capture her, who would have done harm to her as well as others.

Carth spun, kicking out with her left heel, driving towards his chest. He wasn't able to block it, and he staggered back from her attack.

With an angry stare, Carth approached. The magical explosion had injured him.

A look of grim determination crossed his face. He reached into his pocket and pulled out a small glass jar containing a white powder.

Carth's eyes widened as he reached inside it.

"Yes. You recognize this, don't you? We call this

moon dust in my homeland." He cocked his head to the side, the grin still plastered on his face. "Such a mystical name for something with such practical purposes. This is nothing more than a simple combination of plants. Mixed in the right combination, it steals away even the most powerful magical practitioner's ability. As you have seen."

Carth backed away. "Why are you doing this?"

"This? This is for me. There are too many with powers who exist in the world."

"So you intend to capture those with abilities?"

"Only some. Those I take to study. It's important, I think, to understand the source of their powers. Once I understand them, then I can defeat them. And that knowledge is valuable to the right buyer. Now that you reveal yourself, I have seen something like what you possess. You clearly come from the north. There they possess a strange shadow magic. I have seen that from some before. This other—this heat—I have not experienced before. I will study you. I will learn its secrets. Then I will understand how to defeat it."

Carth stood in the corner of the room, her arm weighing heavy, fire burning through it. A part of her hoped that her magic healed her as she stood there. She needed to stall him and prevent him from using this moon dust against her. If she didn't, she suspected he would disable her abilities. Then it would come down to hand-to-hand combat.

Though she had trained with A'ras, she didn't like

her odds against him while injured. She had seen the way he had disabled her fairly easily.

"I'm not the only one with this ability," Carth said.

Let them think that there were others who could come for her. The A'ras might remain in Nyaesh, but that didn't mean they would always remain there. Then there were the descendants of Lashasn. She hoped to organize them and get them trained, but it would take time for them to gain much strength and skill. If someone developed a way to counteract their abilities before they mastered them, they would be defenseless.

The scholar stalked towards her, holding a handful of the dust now.

What could she do to defend herself? If he released the dust into the air, she could only hold her breath so long. Fighting him would be difficult if she couldn't breathe.

Was there another way?

She still had her abilities. They hadn't been suppressed yet.

A plan began forming in her mind.

The scholar stalked towards her, clearly believing that he had won. He brought his hands together, and the dust hung in the air like a white fog.

"Breathe it in, little soldier of night. There's nowhere for you to go."

Carth closed her eyes, her breath held. He was right. There was no place for her to go. But there was something she could do.

Mixing the shadow and the flame together, she breathed out, much like what Ras had done when she had faced him. The combination of the two met the dust, and it began sizzling, crackling in the air. The moon dust exploded in the air and threw Chathem backward.

That had been unexpected.

Carth still didn't breathe, but launched herself forward, reaching the scholar before he had a chance to recover. She rained blows down on his face. She wasn't willing to kill him; she needed his knowledge.

At first, he managed to withstand her punches, but she began imbuing them with the strength of the shadows. They made her stronger, and each punch came like stone.

His head sagged to the side, and he stopped moving.

Carth wanted to relax; she wanted to sink to the ground and sleep. The energy she used had nearly been overwhelming and was more than she had used at one time in quite a while. She didn't dare relax.

How many others were with him? He had mentioned that he studied on behalf of someone else. She needed to know who before doing whatever it was she would ultimately do with them.

Grabbing him by one foot, she dragged him back towards the door, through it and through the collection of imprisoned women. They glanced at her but said nothing, showing no reaction. The most that anyone reacted was when she pulled open the door leading back into the healer's shop. One of the women let out a soft sigh.

Carth pulled the man into the shop and left the other door open.

She leaned against the door frame, finally daring to take a breath. The man groaned, and she kicked him, knocking him out once more. He stopped moving, blood trickling down his cheeks from where she had struck him.

She felt no remorse.

Carth dragged him around the corner, reaching the front of the shop, where she stopped and looked up. A dazed expression came over her at what she saw.

"Guya?"

CHAPTER 27

CARTH BLINKED, TRYING TO CLEAR THE CONFUSION FROM her mind. After using her power as much as she had, the fatigue was nearly overwhelming. She wanted to sleep, but how could she after everything she had been through?

How was it possible that Guya stood before her?

And how was it that he looked unharmed?

She had seen the trail of blood. They had followed it.

The small healer she had seen when she'd first brought Dara to the shop sat in a chair. She had her hands folded in her lap, and she wore a tight smile on her face. Her eyes fixed on Carth, unblinking.

"Interesting. Moon dust usually sedates everyone."

"I told you she would be difficult to suppress," Guya said.

Carth looked from Guya to the small woman, looking for Timothy. Where had the mercenary gone?

Her gaze fell upon the crumpled form of a body in the corner. She noted his sword lying just out of reach. There were no others in the room.

Had there been others when Timothy had come in here?

She thought there had been, but then again, she'd thought they wouldn't face anything more difficult than a small healer.

"Why are you doing this, Guya?" Carth asked.

Guya looked at her but didn't speak.

The healer stood, leaning on her chair for support. "When he said you were strong, I didn't think it possible that you were quite this strong. You escaped when you should not have been able to. And managed to convince that one"—she motioned to Timothy where he lay on the ground—"to join your cause. An interesting thing you managed to do."

Carth started backing towards the door, but she felt movement behind her. She didn't dare turn around. If she did, what would she find?

She reached for her connection to the shadows, pulling on that as well as on her connection to the flame. She used those connections to help her understand how many were behind her. She counted three, primarily through the way they pressed upon her weakened connection to the flame. Movement against the shadows told her there was probably another one. Why wasn't she able to detect them with the flame?

Questions for later.

She wouldn't be escaping through the back door.

Chathem began moaning. She kicked at him again, not wanting him to waken. After what she'd gone through stopping him the first time, she didn't dare risk it a second.

"Why did you return here?" the woman asked.

Guya answered for her. "She came for her friend."

Carth glared at him. After everything she had been through with him? She had thought Guya a friend. "I would've come for you as well."

Guya shook his head. "You care for the women. I've seen how you treat the others. You are predictable, Carth."

"Predictable? Because I wanted to see the Hjan defeated?"

There was a flicker of movement on the woman's face. She recognized the name. She had a connection to the Hjan as well. Was that part of the reason they had betrayed her?

"Why did you come to the north? I thought you weren't a slaver."

Guya's face clouded. "I'm not a slaver."

"You should look back in the back room, then. Seems like there's nearly two dozen women, some barely more than children. I've seen the way they use those women."

Guya shook his head. "Hoga only seeks those with power."

Carth laughed darkly. At least she had a name for this woman. It was an awful thing that they should be betrayed by another woman, and it felt like a larger betrayal than anything else. So often it had been men who had betrayed her. So often it had been men she'd been fighting.

First Felyn, then the attacks within Nyaesh, and even the blood priests. All of them had been men. All of them wanting to torment women.

This Hoga had strength. She must, if she was able to suppress Carth's magic with her concoction of powders, but she should use it to prevent others from suffering. And yet she did not. She did nothing more than allow other women to suffer.

"How could you?" she asked the woman.

Hoga studied her but said nothing.

"If you're so concerned about slavers, why are you with her?" Carth asked Guya.

Hoga frowned. "What choice do you think he has? Do you think all of this simply a game for him?"

A game was an interesting choice of words. Guya knew that she played Tsatsun, and she knew he had some skill, but he was not at the same level as her.

Carth shook away the thoughts and glared at Hoga and Guya. "Tell me where to find Dara, and I might not destroy you completely."

Hoga leaned forward. "Is that what you think this

is? Do you believe this to be a negotiation?" She waved her hand around her. "Look at the others here with us. Do you think they will simply let you depart?"

Carth kept her eyes fixed on Guya. "I don't need the others. All I need is Guya. The rest of you will die."

Carth exploded out with the remaining power she had contained.

At the same time, Hoga brought her hands over her head and swirled them around her. Pale white dust drifted into the air.

Moon dust.

Carth couldn't let it affect her. If she got too close, she ran the risk of losing the ability to use her magic. She had little doubt that Hoga would be more skilled than the other man had been.

But she would use her power differently.

She wrapped the shadows around her, creating a fog.

It came on so thick—so dense—there was no way the others would be able to see through it. She added a hint of the flame, surging enough that it would burn off the moon dust, praying that what had worked last time would work again.

She lunged forward, knowing through the shadows and the connection to the flame where to find the others in the room. If she was right, she would be the only one able to detect them.

She caught the men behind her first.

She struck with her knife, slashing, catching one in

the stomach and the next two in the chest. Each grunted and then fell, dropping before her.

She spun, turning towards where she detected Guya.

She kicked, catching him on the side of the head, and he made a soft noise as she struck him. She fought through the memory of what they'd been through, how he had been her friend and had worked with her, helping—or so she'd thought.

He had betrayed her. And if he had, it was Guya's fault that Dara had been sick. It would be Guya's fault that Dara had been abducted—that *Carth* had been abducted.

Guya fell.

She kicked again, driving shadows through her leg, granting them strength, and he stopped moving.

Then she turned her attention to the woman.

Where was she? Through the shadows and with her flame, she couldn't detect her.

Had she disappeared? Carth had started towards the others first, and maybe she should have focused on Hoga.

She lowered the shadows.

Looking around, Carth surveyed the inside of the shop and found it empty other than those who had been here before.

She cursed softly to herself. She had lost Hoga.

She looked down to Guya and then back to the

other man she'd captured. She might've lost Hoga, but she might have a way to find her again.

Carth steadied her breathing, slowing her mind as she had long ago learned to do when playing the game Tsatsun. This game would be important, not only for her but for those she cared about.

If she failed, her friends would suffer.

If she failed, it was possible that Dara might die.

A plan began to come into focus. Not only a plan, but a sequence of moves, one that, if she played it right, would force Hoga to play the game Carth wanted her to play. It would have to work.

For her to recover her friends, it would have to work.

CHAPTER 28

CARTH KNELT IN FRONT OF GUYA ON THE *GOTH SPALD*, waiting for him to awaken. She had him strapped to the mast, his arms bound behind him, legs tied together with thick bands of rope. She had the other man she'd faced tied to the railing. Timothy stood over him, his sword unsheathed and his body tensed, as if he were ready to strike.

A deep bruise had formed underneath his eye, and a gash on his cheek had been hastily stitched closed with a length of thread that Carth had found in the healer's shop.

Guya groaned and rolled over, glancing first at her and then over to Timothy. A hint of a smile played at his lips. "Good. I'm glad you managed to get me away from her. Did you release the others?"

"They're free. And safe from you," Carth answered.

"Then we can get on to finding Lindy and—"

Carth kicked him in the side.

Guya doubled over, grunting. The ropes holding him to the mast restricted how far he could bend when she kicked him. She was no longer willing to listen to him and his excuses.

"Where are they?"

Guya shook his head. "I'm not with her. Like I said, release me and I can help you search for Dara."

Carth had been struggling with what had happened to Dara. When she'd gotten sick on the ship, there had been nothing Carth could do for her. Guya had feigned ignorance, when he was the reason that Dara had grown sick.

Seeing Guya with Hoga had answered how. She still didn't understand the *why*, but at least now she understood *who* had poisoned Dara.

"I'm only going to ask you one more time." She unsheathed her knives and began pulling on her powers. As tired as she was, she wasn't sure how much strength she would be able to generate, but she was willing to use all she had left if it meant helping her friends.

She placed the knife against the bare flesh of his forearm. She made a slight cut, barely enough to draw a bead of blood that pooled on the surface of his skin, and pressed out slightly with the shadows.

"Where. Are. They?"

Guya's eyes remained fixed on the knife. He had seen her use it brutally before, so she didn't need to threaten him with what she was capable of doing with it. The threat came from what else might happen were she to unleash the shadows. She didn't think he had any abilities, not like the Hjan, and not like the blood priest, but the shadows would still consume him.

The friendliness to his face faded, replaced by a hard mask. She hadn't seen that expression before.

Or had she?

When she had first seen Guya, he'd been in the tavern and had drugged Talun. Hadn't she seen him dose others before?

How had she been so foolish? She had trusted Guya because he had sailed with her, because he had been willing to work with her, but what if it had all been an act?

She had thought herself skilled at reading others, but here was a man who had somehow managed to betray her for a long time.

"She knows about the *Goth Spald*. They will come for me."

Carth took her knife and jabbed into his shoulder. She ignored his cry of pain as she sent a surge of flame through it. Withdrawing her knife, she wiped it on his sleeve before standing and sheathing at.

"We need answers, you can't kill him," Timothy said.

Carth shook her head. "I don't intend to kill him. I also don't want him to pose a risk for us if they do happen to attack."

Timothy motioned towards the other bound man

with his sword. "What about this one? Why is he with them?"

"Who is that?" Carth asked Guya.

Guya's gaze drifted towards Chathem, and he shrugged. "Just another hired hand."

Carth knew that wasn't the truth. The man had been not only skilled but also knowledgeable. This wasn't a man who had simply been hired for a job. He wasn't a mercenary like Timothy, skilled with the sword but unlikely to be plugged in deeper. This man was a part of whatever Guya had been a part of.

"Try again."

Guya looked up at her, his eyes narrowing, his brow furrowing as anger surged from him. "This has nothing to do with you. All they needed was power. I wasn't going to involve you." His eyes narrowed, and either sadness or anger surged within them. "You could've been free. I've seen the way you fight, what you've done. I wasn't willing to put you at risk, and I tried to keep you from this. But you had to press."

"You tried to keep me from this? You drugged Dara, making her sick so that we needed the help of a healer who would then capture her? That's not the sign of anyone who was trying to keep me out of it. You know I would do anything for my friends."

"No. I've seen you do anything for Ih-lash. I've seen you do anything for the A'ras. You don't have any friends, Carth."

Carth clenched her jaw, resisting the urge to strike

him. It would accomplish nothing, and would probably not even make her feel better. She was angry enough at the fact that she hadn't caught on to Guya and his betrayal. She wouldn't let him goad her into something else.

"What is Dara to you?" Carth asked him. "Why capture her? Why not Lindy first?"

"Lindy is..." He shook his head, and for a moment Carth wondered if he would answer.

Then Guya took a deep breath, forced a dark smile and jerked on the ropes holding his wrists behind him bound to the mast. When he didn't get himself free, he relaxed.

He attempted to look casual, in spite of his bindings. "Lindy is not nearly as valuable as Dara. Dara has a different kind of skill."

"It wasn't her skills you were looking for. You intended to use her for whatever sort of slavery these men intended. You were going to force her into service as"—Carth almost couldn't bring herself to say it, but she owed it to Dara to do so—"a prostitute. That's what you wanted her for."

Guya granted and shook his head. "If you know anything about me, you would know that is not what I'm interested in."

"What, then? You think I should believe that you had some other benevolent purpose for Dara? After poisoning her in such a way that she was so sick that we had to bring her to your 'healer'?"

"I did what I had to in order to find answers. You aren't the only one who wants to stop the Hjan."

Carth paced around the mast, keeping Guya in her sight. She had a pair of knives unsheathed as she paced, thinking about what she would do with him. She could leave him bound, or better yet, leave him crippled and toss him into the sea. It was fitting for a sailor like him, someone who believed in the justice of the sea.

But a part of her questioned. Guya hadn't always been deceptive, had he? Was it possible that he was only interested in stopping the Hjan?

She thought of the powders and medicines Hoga had possessed. Something like those would be valuable when faced with the Hjan. The Hjan had abilities that gave them great power, and they were in a land now where the Hjan were more prevalent. This was a place where they would be more likely to attack.

"Who is she?" Carth asked as she made her circle around the mast. She stopped in front of Guya and knelt down so that she got close enough to meet his eyes. "Who is she to you?"

Guya met her gaze and said nothing.

"What did they do to you?"

Guya took a small breath, glaring at her. "The north has only begun to understand what the Hjan will do. They have only begun to understand how dangerous they are. Here in Asador, we know. We have lived under the threat of the Hjan for far too long. Long enough to know—"

Carth stood. The sound of boots on the dock caught her attention.

She kicked Guya in the temple, knocking him out once more, and raced over to Timothy.

He stood at the railing, peering down into the darkness, eyes searching along the dock.

"What did you hear?" he asked.

"Footsteps," she whispered.

As she pulled on the shadows, dispelling the darkness, she detected nearly a dozen people along the dock. She swore softly under her breath.

Timothy glanced over at her. "How many?"

"A dozen."

If they were a dozen like Hoga, or even a dozen like the man tied to the railing, that might be more than she could stop, even using her powers; their ability to counter her made them dangerous.

She still hadn't gotten answers from Guya. And maybe given what he had done to her, the way he had betrayed her, he wouldn't give her answers.

Staying here put them at risk.

She sliced through the ropes binding Chathem to the railing. Using the shadows, she lifted him to her shoulder and stepped across the ship to the other side. Searching the dock there, she saw no sign of anyone else.

"Where you going?"

"Somewhere else. I need answers."

Timothy nodded. "I'm coming with you."

Carth smiled grimly, and when Chathem started moaning, she struck him in the back of the head with her knife, knocking him out once more. He stopped moving, and she jumped, disappearing into the darkness below.

CHAPTER 29

THE INSIDE OF THE TAVERN WAS LESS RAUCOUS THAN THE last time Carth had been there. She looked around, searching for familiar face, keeping Chathem leaning against her, hoping that he appeared nothing more than an intoxicated man. Timothy sat next to her, his hand gripping the other's back, keeping him propped upright so that they could look for the barmaid Carth had met here last time.

"Why this place?" Timothy asked.

Other than the *Goth Spald*, she didn't have anywhere else to go. She wasn't willing to tell Timothy that. He didn't need to know that after everything they had gone through, she was unprepared to find the answer she needed.

Worse, she had left Guya bound on the ship. He shouldn't be able to find her—this was the place she had come with Lindy—but she had no idea if he had been following her, or if he'd sent others to follow her. Now she felt truly isolated.

"There are other ways to find information." Timothy's eyes took in all of the tavern, searching around him with an observant gaze.

Carth nodded. There would be other ways to find information, but in a town like Asador, one she was not familiar with, taverns were the places she defaulted to. What better way for her to obtain information than from a woman who lived in the midst of it?

Julie appeared from behind a door leading to the back of the tavern. Carth nodded to Chathem. "Watch him?"

Timothy nodded his head in a quick agreement. Carth stood and hurried towards the back of the tavern, where Julie started to make the rounds. She caught Julie by the wrist, and the woman turned to her, eyes widening when she saw her.

"You."

"What about me?" Carth asked. Julie glanced around the tavern before her gaze settled on Timothy, with the other man propped against him. Her eyes widened slightly.

"You recognize him, don't you?" Carth said.

Julie motioned her to follow. She weaved through the tavern, making her way towards the back, to the door leading to the kitchen. Carth followed closely, keeping her eyes on her, afraid to let her get too far away, still not certain whether Julie would attempt to run or say something.

Once inside the kitchen, Carth glanced around. There was a certain sensation that came to her from being within the kitchen of a tavern. It reminded her of Vera and the time she had spent with her. She didn't think of Vera too often these days, but that had been the first stable place she'd had after her parents were killed. Vera had always treated her well. And Carth appreciated that from her.

The inside of the kitchen smelled of baking bread and roasting meats and vegetables, all smells that Carth was familiar with from her time in Nyaesh. More than that, it made her mouth water, reminding her of how hungry she was.

"It's your fault," Julie started. "You had to go after Terran. Because of you, they took—"

"I found her. She's safe."

Julie blinked. "You found her?"

"They didn't bring her from the city. She's safe."

"Safe?"

Carth nodded. "Help me, and I'll show you how to find her."

"What kind of help?"

"I need to find Terran."

Julie sighed. "That will only lead to danger."

"I know. But I *will* find him." Her stomach rumbled again.

"How long has it been since you had a good meal?"

Julie arched an eyebrow. "If you're hungry, you don't have to have your stomach growl at me."

She turned to a pot and began scooping heaping spoonfuls onto a plate. She handed this to Carth, setting a spoon in her other hand.

Carth could only stare at her, mouth agape. This wasn't what she had expected, though she wasn't sure what she had expected.

"Last I heard from you was when you planned to go after the missing women."

Carth took a spoonful of the stew, letting it fill her mouth with flavor. She nodded. "I did. I had to, since no one else would do anything." She took another few bites. Julie stood there watching her, her face unreadable. "I was captured."

She took another few bites of the stew, her mouth watering with each one, eating until her stomach began to finally settle.

Julie stood back and simply watched Carth eat.

When her stomach was full, Carth shook herself. "Thank you." It was strange for her to experience such kindness. After the torment she'd been through, all the suffering she had dealt with after being captured, drugged and attacked, it meant a lot to her to be shown some kindness.

"There wasn't anything we *could* do. All we wanted was to find them and see if there was anything we could do to bring them back home. So many have been lost from here."

They could have done more, but Carth wouldn't push that now. "Do you know why?"

Julie shook her head. "Women have been taken from the city for many years. We haven't known where they went, only that they would disappear. We've never discovered where they've gone, or who took them. Others have searched for answers, but haven't been able to find anything."

Carth studied her. "Others?"

"There are those who work to keep these women safe. We've tried for many years to stem the tide of disappearances, but we've failed. Then you come into town. You disrupt attacks that have taken place. You seem as if you actually want to help. It's something we are unaccustomed to here."

Carth frowned. "I do want to help and have been trying to since I first came to town. First by trying to find my friend, and then, when I was captured along with her, I did what I could to help the others I found. We rescued them and left them in a village, safe from those who would harm them."

Julie's breath caught. "How many others?"

"Nearly one hundred," Carth said. "There were men, slavers, who wanted to harm them, but we kept them safe, preventing the slavers from reaching them."

"And where are these slavers now?"

Carth nodded to the other room. "There's one out there. He thought to attack me, but he wasn't alone.

There were others with him. I intend to find out what he knows and stop the others."

Julie stared at Carth. "You… you did it."

"Did what?"

Julie stepped away from the counter, and Carth realized she had a knife clutched in her hand. It was a simple kitchen knife, one that could do damage but was not meant to be a weapon. It was an instrument, nothing more.

"Julie?"

The other woman looked to Carth, almost dragging her gaze away from the doorway into the kitchen. "We've not discovered the key to the network. We always knew there was one. It's been more than Terran."

"The key was Hoga."

Julie blinked. "Hoga?"

"You know her." Carth wasn't surprised that she knew of Hoga. The woman was a healer, and there likely weren't many to be found in the city.

"How could she?" Julie wondered aloud.

Carth shook her head. There were no answers as to why, or how. All she knew was what had happened.

"Hoga lost her own daughter to an attack long ago. Her son left seeking vengeance…"

Carth closed her eyes. Son? A missing daughter?

They fell into her mind like pieces on a game board. Could it be that everything Hoga did was for revenge?

Worse, was it possible that Guya sought revenge for his sister?

It almost made her feel remorse for stabbing him. Almost.

He had still betrayed them. Had he asked her for help, had he only come to her when he'd learned about what she could do, she would have been compelled to try and help him. As it was, now there was little reason for her to help him, other than for the fact that she understood the need for vengeance against the Hjan.

"Was her son a man named Guya?" Carth asked Julie.

Julie's eyes widened slightly. "You know him, don't you? Wait… is his ship the one you came to Asador on?"

Carth sighed. "Unfortunately, it is. He betrayed me. Us."

At least now she understood the why, but she still didn't know what had happened to her friends. She still didn't understand how Hoga had captured Dara… and Lindy now. But she understood why. Hoga wanted to use them, study their abilities, and find a way to counter them.

Carth understood that—could actually get behind it —but betraying her as Guya had done, she didn't understand.

"I need your help."

Julie nodded. "Anything. I will help."

"I need answers. I need information about how to find Hoga and what she intends to do next."

"She wouldn't leave her shop. Almost as much as her children, her shop is everything to her."

Carth's brow furrowed. After rescuing the other women, she had left the healer's shop empty, dragging Guya and the other man away. Had she given Hoga the way back?

But then, Carth understood why she would value her shop as much as she did, if it contained all the powders and other items she needed in order to mix the right concoctions to counter magic.

Hoga's attachment to the shop was much like Guya's attachment to his ship.

With that realization, she wondered how Hoga would react if her shop was taken from her.

She might have a way to bargain for her friends. It would require her to be ruthless, but after what she had been through, what Hoga had put others through, Carth decided that the woman deserved ruthlessness.

CHAPTER 30

Carth crept along the street outside the healer's shop. She shrouded herself in shadows, keeping herself concealed, for the most part. She resisted the urge to retreat too deeply into the shadows, knowing that if she were to do so, she would expend more energy than what was safe. After the constant fighting today, she feared expending too much energy. She still didn't know what she might encounter with Hoga.

The windows of the shop were darkened. The yellow door was shut and Carth imagined it was locked as well. She waited alone. Timothy had chosen to remain with Chathem, telling her that the scholar was part of *his* assignment. It was for the best. This was something she needed to do herself.

All she needed was to draw out Hoga. Then she could find out where the woman had kept Lindy and

Dara, rescue them, and destroy what Hoga planned. That was all she could think about at this point.

Still... still, she kept her focus on her next move, and the one after, and multiple moves beyond that. If she took her focus off the endgame, she risked getting outmaneuvered. Already she feared that she had made mistakes in how she played.

Cloaked by the shadows as she was, she felt a hint of movement. It was subtle, and had she not practiced with drawing on the shadows to use them to detect movement, she doubted she would have been able to pick it up.

Carth slipped forward, reaching the door to the shop. If necessary, she was prepared to explode outward with heat and fire, destroying the shop to draw Hoga out.

The shadow cloaking failed.

It happened without warning.

One moment she was holding on to the shadows, cloaked within them, and the next moment they were gone.

It felt as if they were torn from her. It was painful, but she still could reach them, though she was weakened, drained from the effort of what had happened. She could still reach the edge of the shadows and could still pull on it, but her attempts to do anything more with it were unsuccessful.

Carth looked up and down the street, searching for

signs of Hoga or any who were with her. There was no sign of anyone.

That meant inside the shop.

If they could tear her shadows away from her so easily, they had come up with a way to counter them without dosing her with powders. Had they managed the same with her connection to the flame?

Carth reached for her S'al magic.

She exploded it out from herself, hitting the door to the shop. When it struck, she raced forward, driving her heel through the handle of the door.

Without intending to, she had used the shadows as well.

They weren't restricted from her, and she could use the shadows for strength and speed. The combined magic allowed her to shatter the door.

Inside the shop, she took a quick survey. She saw no sign of Hoga or any of the others.

A slight haze hung in the air. Carth resisted taking a deep breath, afraid that Hoga had set a trap for her. She focused on the fire and pressed out with an explosion that ripped through the shop. Carth turned her attention to the rows of medicines. The dried leaves, berries, and various oils ignited quickly, the flames racing through them. Fire quickly engulfed the entire interior of the shop.

The pressure preventing her from using her shadow magic remained.

Whatever it was that Hoga did to her, she hadn't stopped her yet.

She turned towards the back of the shop.

She glanced at the door leading to the alleyway, for a moment considering going through it and searching for Hoga there, but there would be no place for her to hide in the alley.

She then turned her attention to the next room, the one where she had discovered the captives. A question came to her: why had Hoga held these women here?

Carth didn't believe she wanted to use the women as prostitutes. What purpose would there be in that if she really sought revenge for what the Hjan had done? She cared about studying those with power.

Was that why they had claimed Dara?

Why not Lindy then as well?

Carth paused in this room, noting traces of fire and a hint of chemical odor here as well.

They hadn't been just captive women. They had been women with abilities.

That had to have been the reason Hoga had kept them here.

Carth had freed them, released them back into the city, but had that been the right move?

She used the power of her flame magic and surged through the room, letting fire engulf it as well.

Racing through the door leading to the office space, Carth paused. Inside here, she noted evidence of recent activity. Furniture that had been knocked down in the fight had since been set back upright. The damage to the room had been repaired.

Carth hesitated, heart racing, thinking about where Hoga might have gone. If this shop was like the *Goth Spald* was to Guya, she wouldn't have left it.

But were the medicines in the outer shop truly her prized possessions?

Might there not be another section to her shop? There certainly was another doorway.

Pushing open the door, she headed into a darkened hallway.

Behind her she detected the power of the fire that she had lit, now engulfing the entirety of the shop. She kept it confined to the walls of the shop, commanding the flames to burn out once the contents of the shop were consumed.

That wasn't the only sense of heat she noted.

There was movement down the hallway in the distance. Carth reached for the shadows but still felt resistance. She might be able to use them for strength and stamina, but anything more than that was restricted from her.

Carth made her way down the hall. At the next door, she paused before throwing it open.

A narrow room greeted her. A door on the opposite end waited. She stepped inside, and as she did, she tripped, an unseen line catching her legs.

A bucket fell from the ceiling. Powder sprayed across her.

Carth rolled. She knew better than to breathe in, just as she knew better than to panic. That was what Hoga wanted from her.

How could she have gotten caught in such a simple trap? But, as she knew, sometimes the simplest solutions were the most effective.

Closing her eyes, she focused on her skin, letting the flame race over her, consume the powder that now coated her skin.

It began to sizzle, a hot fire coursing over her skin.

She had learned that her own flame magic would not impact her the same as it did others. The power of her own magic would not burn her.

She didn't breathe as power surged from her.

Then the powder was gone, burned off.

Carth got to her feet, pulling on the shadows, using them to sustain her.

She reached the next door and kicked it, driving shadow and flame magic through her body as she did, throwing the door off its hinges.

Another office greeted her on the side. Carth hesitated, looking to see if there was another trap before deciding to simply ignite the room. Flames raced through it, exploding pockets of powder she hadn't seen.

Carth went through the room into the next room. As with the last, she opened the door, and as soon as she did, a sword swept towards her head. Carth had expected something, but the sword nearly caught her off guard.

She dropped, rolling to the side, swinging her heel around. It collided with her attacker's knee. Connected to the shadows as she rolled, he caved backwards, crumpling.

It was the large man from the forest.

Magic wouldn't work on him, but could it work *around* him?

She had to end this quickly. Delay would only lead to her injury. He was much too large for her to handle otherwise, and he was immune to her magic.

She lit the floor on fire.

The man screamed.

She flipped around, stabbing with her knife, sending out a surge of fire and flame that caught him in the chest.

Carth didn't have a chance to question her actions. Another attacker reached her.

This time, Carth jumped over him and kicked him in the back as she landed. She flipped forward again, her knife connecting and stabbing him in the back, the power of the flame roaring from it.

Would another attack come?

She waited, but none did.

Carth reached the next door and opened it more carefully than the others.

No sword met her.

Instead, she was greeted by six attackers. One of

them raised his hands to toss powder. To others held crossbows. The remaining three stood behind them, swords in hand.

Carth couldn't wait. She pressed out with the flame, igniting the air itself.

Men screamed.

She ignored it, darting in with her knives, slashing through them, ignoring burning flames.

Once through the next door, Carth braced for the next attack, but it never came. The room was empty. There was no trap, no attackers, and no sign of Hoga.

Nothing but solid walls greeted her. Either she was trapped... or there was a way out that she hadn't discovered.

She focused on the power of the flame, using it as well as the shadows to reach for connections to others, but she detected none in the room. There was something about the room itself that she could feel, and frowned.

As she did, a section of the wall slid open. Guya emerged, two swords unsheathed in his hands, the injury that she'd inflicted healed since she'd left him bound to the *Spald*. "I'm sorry, Carth. But this is the end."

Carth took a deep breath, sighing. "I'm sorry, too."

Then she jumped forward and attacked someone she had considered a friend.

CHAPTER 31

CARTH ROLLED FORWARD, SLASHING UP WITH HER KNIVES toward Guya, but not certain what to expect from him. She had never seen him fight in person. Whenever they'd faced any danger, he had remained on the ship, and she'd always been the one to attack. Somehow, she wasn't surprised to discover that he was skilled with the sword.

Guya slashed with his sword and attacked with a tight efficiency. He was good, much better than she had expected, though considering the leisurely way he'd always worn the sword, she should have expected that from him.

"You don't have to do this. You can help me."

Guya shook his head. "If I help you, those I care about will suffer. Why else do you think I was willing to do this?"

He pulled two fistfuls of white powder from his pockets and tossed them into the air.

Carth had been prepared.

She reached through her connection to the flame and let that power explode away from her, igniting the powder in the air.

She focused on his pockets and sent flames toward him.

The powder hidden within his pockets exploded, tearing his pants free.

He stood in front of her in his small clothes, sword still clutched in his hand. A small smile spread across his face. "I didn't think that was what you were interested in. Thought with the way you collected women—"

Carth stabbed forward with her knives and struck him in the shoulder, sending shadows pouring through them.

The power of the shadows incapacitated Guya, and he dropped to the ground, convulsing. Carth took a step back from him, watching for a minute. When he didn't get up, she approached carefully.

She stopped in front of him, looking down, unable to hide the anger on her face, or in her voice. "We were friends. I would've done anything to help protect you, the same as I would've done for Dara and Lindy."

Guya stared up at her. His hands clenched and unclenched and the rest of his body strained, as if trying to move, but dark lines of shadow worked beneath his skin, unleashed by Carth's connection. She let out a sigh.

"Redeem yourself. Where are they?"

Guya stared straight ahead. "You won't find them," he said through clenched teeth.

Carth watched him, and then she sent a surge of blackness through him so that he convulsed one more time. This time, he collapsed and did not arise again.

She looked around the room. What she needed was some sign of Hoga, but there was none. Guya's presence told her that the woman had intended to protect this place, only what was she trying to protect?

She searched Guya's pockets, coming up with a small key as well as a few vials of different-colored powders. She pocketed those, thinking that she would study them later. If there was some way to counter her ability, and counter those with other abilities, it was possible that she could use this and take what Guya and Hoga had learned and apply it towards stopping the Hjan.

Behind a long curtain, she discovered a door. Carth pulled it open carefully and stretched out using the shadows and the flame, searching for evidence of anyone else on the other side. As she did, she found no sign of anyone on the other side of the door.

Carth entered carefully.

She made her way down a wide hallway. Paneled walls rose on either side of her, inset with a few unlit lanterns. Carth took the time to light them with her connection to the flame as she went. A few paintings hung along the wall, skillfully made and reminding her of those she had seen in Nyaesh, near the Hall of Masters.

Towards the end of the hall, there was nothing. The hall simply ended.

There had to be something here.

Carth closed her eyes. She stretched out, probing for signs of others, suspecting that there had to be someone here. As she did, she felt the distinct sense of dozens near her.

Not near her. They were below her.

Carth studied the long carpet running along the hallway. Grasping the end of it, she threw it back and saw three separate hatches cut into the ground. Carth grabbed at the edge of one of them and pulled. Stairs led below.

She went down a couple stairs, then paused, using her abilities to search for signs of anyone hidden in the darkness. She detected something, but it wasn't exactly clear what it was. Not the distinct sense of dozens of other people she had felt when she'd been standing above.

This wasn't the right opening.

She took the stairs back up. The air in the hall had changed. There was a slight floral aroma to it, one that hadn't been here when she had stood here before —had it?

Carth didn't want to take the time to determine if

there was something she had missed. She needed to move quickly now.

She reached the next hatch and struggled to grab an edge. There was a tighter seal with the floor than with the other. Leveraging her knife between the cracks, she propped it up. Borrowing strength from the shadows, she managed to pull the hatch free from the floor and tossed it to the side.

No stairs led below. This was an opening, but one that had no signs of any way to reach the bottom.

Carth surged flame away from her, lighting the space beneath the floor. Darkness stretched away, with no sign of anything more.

This didn't appear to be the place she sought either.

A single opening remained.

The only way she could tell this one was here was by the slight changing of color along the edge of the floorboards. Even her knife struggled to find a gap to pry open.

She sat back and studied it, trying to find a different way in.

Could she try another tactic?

Carth jabbed her shadow knife into the floorboard, piercing deeply. She pulled on it, and with a groan, the board separated from the rest of the floor.

Carth wiggled her knife free and kept it in hand.

Much like the first opening, a set of stairs led down. Shadows shifted in the distance below. The sense of the others she felt against the shadows pulled more strongly here.

Carth took the stairs down, hurrying two at a time. When she reached the bottom, she paused.

There were others in the room now with her.

She didn't see them so much as she felt them. Using another surge of flames, she illuminated the space below. There was resistance to the power of her flame, the kind of resistance that came from somebody with abilities.

Carth approached carefully. She detected something familiar.

She eased off her connection to the flame, letting the darkness surround her and pushing out gently with the shadows, feeling a responding surge in return.

"Lindy?"

Barely a few paces from her, someone sucked in a breath. "Carthenne? How is it that you're here? Did she capture you as well?"

Carth reached her and found chains holding her wrists and ankles, binding her in place so that she could barely move. Carth severed these using a surge through the shadows.

"No."

"The healer is a part of this. Did you know that?"

"I learned too late."

"When you didn't return, I did what I could, but…"

"It doesn't matter. Is Dara here?" She would tell

Lindy about Guya later. She didn't need to know about that until they were safe… and free.

"She was. There are others who—"

"I know. They intend to study you," she said while examining Lindy for injuries. She found nothing obvious as she ran her fingers along Lindy's arms, shoulders, and then down her legs. "Can you help me with them?"

"There are too many. I don't think we can get free."

"Leave that to me."

"You don't understand, Carth. They have something they do that prevents me from even using my shadows. These others, they have abilities as well that have been suppressed."

"I know. As soon as we're free, I'll make sure that it ends."

"How do you plan on doing that?" Lindy asked.

Carth breathed out, using a mixture of shadows and flame so that it hung suspended in the air, burning away some of the barely seen powder suspended there. She understood how Hoga had suppressed their abilities even while these women were captured. It was even worse than the way the slavers had suppressed her abilities. There had been deception, sneaking it into her water or forcing it down her throat while she was incapacitated. This was in the air, forcing them to breathe it in.

"I'm going to capture Hoga, and then she's going to help us."

CHAPTER 32

As they made their way through the lower level of the healer's shop, Carth realized there were connections not visible from above. What would happen if she were to continue wandering? Would she eventually reach the same place where she had initially been captured?

Was that how they moved women out of the city?

Lindy followed her, staying close to her side. Her eyes had a haunted expression to them, one that hadn't been present the last time Carth had seen her. What had happened during her captivity? What had Hoga done to her friend? What would Dara be like when they found her?

"Where do you think they took Dara?" Carth asked Lindy.

Lindy looked over and shook her head. The darkness around them practically enveloped her. She was sinking into the shadows, cloaking herself, hiding even from Carth. "I don't know. They took her away, and I haven't seen her since."

Carth glanced back at the women trailing them. They had nearly two dozen women, many with obvious abilities. Several were shadow blessed. That had surprised Carth. None had any of the abilities of Lashasn. Was that why Dara had been taken?

Some had less obvious abilities, though Carth was surprised to note that two of the women had deep green eyes. They reminded her of the Hjan she had seen several times, and stories she'd heard of the city to the south. It seemed more than coincidental.

They continued onward in silence. Carth debated taking them through the upper levels of the shop, but now that she had destroyed it, she didn't want to risk going back through. She suspected there was another way out this way, and if so—and if she could find it—she would be able to bring these women to safety.

At least, some form of safety.

To find real safety, she would need something else.

The cave changed, becoming rockier, now seemingly cleaved from the walls of the hillside. As it did, Carth became more and more convinced that she headed in the correct direction.

When the hall branched, she paused.

Lindy stood at her shoulder, peering up and down the hall with Carth, neither of them quite certain where to go. In the distance, Carth detected a change in temperature. Would Lindy detect the same, or did Carth only detect it because of her A'ras magic?

She motioned for them to follow her where the heat shifted the most, dropping off. If she was right, this would lead out of the tunnel, and perhaps past the area where she had been captured before.

From there, Carth needed to find some way of reaching Hoga. She still wasn't sure what she would have to do when she found her. Would it matter that she had left Guya for dead?

The farther she walked, the more she detected a salty scent in the air and knew she headed in the right direction.

Carth reached the end of the cavern and found nothing but a rocky wall. Lindy beat on the wall before looking to Carth with her eyes still wide and haunted. "There's no way for us to get out, is there?"

Carth reached through her connection to both the shadows and the flame and pushed away from her, letting the power slide distantly from her. There was an opening on the other side of the wall, but there seemed no way to reach it.

She needed more power than she could draw on her own.

The shadows would grant strength, and she could use the power of the flame, but she needed a focus.

Carth pulled through her mother's ring, using the focus that had been her first connection to the flame, and sent it at the wall. The rock began to glow softly. Carth pushed more energy through it, building steadily, until the rock began shaking, vibrating with energy.

Carth shoved her shadow knife into the stone, letting the shadows flow from it. The combination of the two exploded out from her.

The sound of the ocean washing beneath her came more clearly. A salty breeze gusted through the open space, and night drifted in.

Lindy wore a relieved expression on her face. Some of the haunted expression remained on her features, but not the way it had.

"I'm getting you to safety. Only a little longer."

Lindy nodded slowly.

Carth started down the rock. As she reached the bottom, she stood only a few feet above the ocean, the waves crashing near her. From here, she could see movements nearby, as well as out in the ocean, as ships made their way into the port of Asador. She let out a sigh, breathing in the salty air.

Behind her, Lindy did the same, though neither of them said anything. The other two dozen women following them did so quietly as well, making their way along the rock. Carth motioned towards a trail that led towards the city.

"This will take you back."

One of the women, a younger girl with pale blond hair and deep blue eyes with a few dark smudges on her cheeks, looked at Carth, her eyes widening. "You're not coming with us?"

Carth met Lindy's eyes. "You need to bring them back into the city. Make sure they're safe. Do you remember the tavern where were you first went?" Lindy nodded. "Julie will keep them safe. There's a man there who will help." She hoped Timothy hadn't left yet.

Lindy opened her mouth as if she were to say something, before clapping it shut once more. "I think I can do that. What are you going to do?"

Carth looked back toward the empty cavern. She needed this to end, and in order for that to happen, she needed to reach Hoga.

"I'm going back."

"Are you sure that's safe?" Lindy asked.

Carth looked at the women making their way along the rock. Some had regained a measure of the confidence she suspected they'd had prior to the attack. Others lingered, taking a more cautious approach. Getting the women to safety was part of what needed to happen.

She thought of what Julie had been through, what the women of the city had feared.

"I'm going to find Dara, and then I'm going to end this. It's something that has to be done. This can't happen again. Never again."

CHAPTER 33

ONCE THE WOMEN WERE SAFELY ON THEIR WAY BACK towards the city, Carth ducked back underneath the rock, moving into the cavern once more. Hoga wouldn't have left her shop, much as Guya wouldn't have left the ship. That meant that she'd overlooked something.

She reached the room where the women had been captive and scanned it again. She saw no sign of anything else here. She hurried back the other way, feeling the effects of her flame magic, the flames already eating through the walls above her.

Where was Hoga?

Searching through the rooms where she'd faced attack after attack, she discovered no sign of her. She made her way back to the room where she'd found three trapdoors in the floor. She'd discovered the women in one, but what of the other two?

Carth jumped down the first one. She ignited the flame through the knife she carried, brightening it so that it would light her way.

The room was a small cavern. Chains were set into the wall, but there was nothing else here that revealed what the room had been used for. Traces of color smeared along the wall, some black, some green, some a sickly brown. The air had a musky and fetid odor. She wondered what Hoga might have used this room for, but given the staining on the walls and the odor present, perhaps this hadn't been where she'd tested her powders to see if there were ways she could counteract abilities.

Carth surged with the power of the shadows and jumped out of the cavern. She made her way to the middle one. Neither of the other caverns had held Hoga. Why should the last one be any different?

The only way she would get answers was by jumping down.

When she did, she saw that the room was appointed differently than the others.

The others had been burrowed from rock, the walls nothing but stone, but this one was different. Instead of nothing but rock, and chains anchored to the walls, there was a desk and a row of shelves.

Carth was studying the shelves when she felt pressure behind her.

She spun, but there was nothing there.

She had detected something, but saw no sign of anyone else. As she started to send power through her knives, she heard a voice above her.

Carth released the shadows and the flame.

She stood holding on to only a trickle. It was barely anything, only enough to avoid having it separated from her, but little enough that someone shouldn't be able to detect it.

"You have failed, Hoga."

"Is that what you believe? I think I've proven that the formula works as I promised. Your man knows what I have done."

Carth crept closer. She recognized Hoga's voice, and there was familiar something about the other voice as well, though she didn't know why it should be.

"Terran will no longer serve in Asador. There have been too many mistakes. You were to find power, not whores."

"I didn't find whores!"

"No. But you failed to inform me when *he* did."

"I can't control how Terran used the others."

"An interesting excuse."

"It's no excuse. It's the truth."

"You will hand over what you've created."

"What of your promise?" Hoga asked.

"I think this was less a promise and more of a bargain, don't you?"

"You will leave us alone here. That was the bargain."

"The agreement was that your powders would work, and if they worked, we would leave the city for now."

"I have proven that they work. We have the other with the same ability! You saw how we kept her captive for—"

Captive.

Did they mean Dara?

"She escaped. I think we've learned that your powders were ineffective. What you've promised has not come to fruition."

Not Dara, then. They meant Carth.

"It was effective while she was taking it. All you must do is suppress her, and her abilities are countered. If you would like me to demonstrate?"

There was a hoarse chuckle.

Carth froze. She recognized that sound.

It was the green-eyed Hjan.

"No, Hoga. I'm not willing to test this."

"Why, Danis, it seems you're afraid of me."

Carth had a name. It was more than she'd ever had before.

"Not afraid. But I've learned to be wary of you and your strange powders. You have some potential, woman. You can serve us well."

"Serve? This was an agreement. This was not serving you."

"I think you will find that you will want to serve us."

Carth had had enough. The Hjan were involved, and Hoga had agreed to work with them. What she didn't know was *why*. She had thought Hoga wanted to prevent the Hjan from attacking. Had she thought to bargain with them?

How was it different than what Carth had done?

It was time for answers, especially as she had the advantage.

Carth surged on the shadows and jumped.

She appeared in the room above, brandishing her knives, and landed behind Hoga. She jabbed the knife into Hoga's back, sending shadows through her—but more controlled than she had with Guya—and she sagged, dropping to the ground.

She held the knives out, turning towards Danis.

He smiled, and his deep green eyes glittered with amusement. He had a long face and a flat expression, and his height alone would have been intimidating. As he had when she'd seen him last, he wore a dark jacket and pants, with a sword hanging at his waist. "Interesting. I had not expected you to linger once you freed slaves."

Carth glared at him. "Slaves? Is that what they are to you?"

Dennis shrugged. "They are but parts of something larger."

"I think you're mistaken. They are under my protection."

"Indeed? And why should that matter?"

"Because you agreed to the Accords, and the Accords grant peace between the A'ras, the Reshian, and the Hjan."

Danis smiled at her, almost a dark sneer to his face. "You think your agreement extends to these girls?"

"Yes."

"They are not Reshian. They are not A'ras. And if I claim them as Hjan, I would not be violating the Accords."

"I claim them."

"Yet the Accords were not signed by you. They were signed between the Reshian and the A'ras."

He was right. She was neither A'ras nor Reshian, though she had forged the Accords on behalf of both. If she couldn't find a way to tie it together and claim the women, she had no way of truly keeping them safe. She didn't trust Danis to leave them alone, which meant she had to do something.

She intended to end the threat of the Hjan, and she still needed to deal with Hoga and the others, but this needed to be dealt with first.

Pieces moved in her mind.

She would make this difficult for Danis.

Carth gripped the hilts of her knives. "If I don't claim them, then the A'ras and the Reshian can't claim me. I am of neither."

Danis's eyes started to darken as the implications of what she had said sank in.

Carth didn't give him a chance to consider it for long.

She laughed at him, surging on shadows, using the power of the flame, sending them through the knives. One knife sucked the darkness from the room while the other blazed brightly. She plunged her flame knife into his side. As she did, she surged through that power, exploding into him.

She expected him to collapse, but he did not.

Danis took a step away from her, a dangerous glint in his eyes.

He flickered.

His skin surged with color, and the blood seeping down his side subsided. Her attack had failed.

Carth slashed forward again, this time using the shadows.

When her knife nicked his skin, she sent the shadows through the blade.

She'd seen how shadows would affect the Hjan, and how they could incapacitate them. It was how she had killed Felyn and the other Hjan in the past.

Danis was different.

She shouldn't have expected anything else. He would be powerful; possibly the most powerful of the Hjan.

Where the shadows had begun working along his skin, they faded quickly.

He looked at her, a smile on his face. "My turn."

He flickered.

Nausea rolled through her. When he reappeared, he was behind her.

Carth spun, catching the sweep of his sword with one of her knives, deflecting it downward. He flickered again, this time appearing on the other side of her. Again she managed to catch his blade and deflect it away.

He flickered again and again, and each time she barely managed to deflect his attack.

Only through the nausea she felt with his flickering was she able to prevent him from connecting.

She wasn't strong enough to stop him, not after all the energy she had expended getting to this point. So much of her power had been used fighting through the upper levels of Hoga's shop, fighting through her powders and her men, even killing a friend.

There had to be something more.

He could counter each magic separately, but could he do the same with both at once?

She focused on the shadows, and on the flame, drawing them into herself. She'd grown much stronger since the last time she'd faced any of the Hjan. She *could* stop him.

Through her focus, she detected where he was moving. Not only where he was, but where he would appear.

The next time he flickered, she was ready.

He appeared, and she struck with both knives, stabbing him in both shoulders. She surged through both shadows and flame as she did. Power flowed into him, pinning him in place. His skin began to discolor, and none of his power was able to stop it.

He screamed.

Carth held the knives buried in his shoulders. Power coursed from her and into him.

He tried flickering, and failed.

Magic surged against her knives, but it failed as well.

"The Accords extend to those I protect."

Danis glared at her with his deep green eyes. "You do not want to make an enemy of the Hjan. You do not want to make an enemy of Venass."

That was a name she had not heard. More questions.

"As I said, the Accords extend to me and those I protect."

She contemplated finishing him. He couldn't move, trapped as he was by her knives, but if she did, how would she keep the others safe? Leaving him alive was the only way she would accomplish what she wanted. It was one move in a longer game, one that was beginning to be much longer than she ever would have imagined. It was the kind of game she feared playing, knowing that real lives were at stake.

She had to hope that he would make the move she anticipated: seek survival.

"And who do you represent?" Danis asked.

"I represent…" She thought about how she would

answer. She had been pressured to join with others in the past but had declined. Was joining the only way she could accomplish what she needed?

If so, it was a shame it had come to this. She could've sided with them long ago.

"The C'than."

Danis's gaze narrowed even more. "You make a mistake, girl."

"This girl is the one who has you trapped. The Accords. They extend to me and those I protect."

"And you are with the C'than?"

Carth nodded.

She could see conflicting emotions across his features. His dark green eyes seemed to flash, and she felt it as he attempted to flicker again but failed.

She held her knives plunged into his shoulders. "I will end you. There will be no further discussion. If you wish to live, the Accords will be extended to those I protect."

Danis nodded once.

"Say it."

"The Accords extend to you, Carthenne Rel of the C'than." Carth wasn't surprised that he knew her full name, and it was the first time someone had ever given her an attribution of a place that she felt was fitting, as much as she had resisted joining.

"I accept." She withdrew her knives.

Danis staggered back. He flashed again, and the

flesh where her knives had penetrated began healing, the shadows fading from his skin.

"You may come to regret your decision, Carthenne Rel of C'than."

"I bought peace. I do not regret that."

"You may regret not killing me."

"I already do."

Danis flashed a dark smile, and nausea struck her as he flickered, disappearing.

Carth let out a deep breath and felt something strike her in the back.

She staggered forward and spun.

Hoga stood across from her, powder suspended in the air.

Carth breathed out shadow and flames, and the powder burned off in an explosion.

Hoga stared at her, eyes wide with surprise. "How did you—"

"You," Carth said, starting towards Hoga and grabbing her by the elbow, "are going to help me."

"With what?"

"With my endgame."

Hoga stared at her, her head tipped to the side. "And what is that?"

"Defeating the Hjan."

"But you just agreed to a treaty."

Carth nodded. "The treaty is for now. Both of us knew it. It buys peace and it buys time. But that one, that man you named as Danis, he will violate it again, if not in fact, then in spirit. I will be ready. You will help."

"How?"

Carth grinned. "With the women you thought to make slaves."

EPILOGUE

CARTH SAT ABOARD THE DECK OF THE *GOTH SPALD*, Lindy sitting on one side of her, Dara—now reclaimed from where Hoga had trapped her—on the other. They had a mug of ale from a keg that had been wheeled aboard by Julie, a gift for all the work Carth had done in saving the women who had been captured throughout Asador.

"When do you want to leave?" Lindy asked.

Carth shook her head. "Not leave. We'll remain here for now. We'll observe. And then…"

Carth had debated what they would end up doing. It had been facing Danis that had convinced her. Now that she had the Accords signed, everyone she placed under her protection would be safe. Not only from women like Hoga, but from the Hjan. That was worth something.

More than that, she could use those she put under

her protection and could gather information. That had been the missing piece all this time.

Julie had taught her how much information could be gleaned from taverns on this continent, much as it could be where she was from. And now, now she would have a network within Asador. From here, she would go other places, establish similar networks, and use them to gain the information she needed to make certain the Hjan didn't violate the treaty, all while readying to take them down.

"But these women…," Lindy started.

"They're stronger than you give them credit for," Carth said.

"There aren't enough. Two dozen women—"

"And another hundred in the village of Praxis." Carth thought about those, and thought about how she would ask them to help her. She had little doubt that they would. Just as she had little doubt that they had some abilities she'd overlooked as well.

From here, she would find where the slavers brought other women. She would sequester them, bring them under protection. She would create a shadow network, and she would bind them together.

It was the sort of thing her mother would've been proud of.

If only Timothy had remained. He had taken Chathem and escorted him from the city. Carth still didn't know why—or where he'd brought the man— only that he was part of Timothy's larger mission. She hoped she would see him again. Were it not for him, she might never have found the women of Praxis.

"And Guya?" Dara asked.

Carth looked at the ship. Guya was gone, his ship now hers. The betrayal had been complete. It pained her that she had needed to end him, but it pained her more that he had betrayed her.

Hoga would be used to create powders and other protective devices that the women could use. She suspected Hoga could also be used to generate powders that would strengthen many of Carth's women. She would use that knowledge. That was the reason Hoga was on the ship.

"Now it's up to us. Guya taught us to sail, and now we'll take his ship. I think it's a reasonable bargain."

Lindy stared at her, mouth agape. "You really intend to do this?"

Carth looked up at the mainmast, thinking of the last time she'd unfurled it, pulling on lines. Guya had taught her to sail, and that had been his mistake. Now she would use his ship to reach the other places where she needed to create her network, one more step along the way to truly defeating the Hjan.

She raised her glass. "For now, we should relax. We've been sick for too long."

Lindy grinned. "I do enjoy sailing."

Dara stared at the mug, her mouth twisted in a grimace. "You go ahead. I'm not sure I'm ready to drink this yet."

"I think we can relax and celebrate. For now."

Carth took a drink, enjoying the flavor of the ale, feeling confident in the move she had made, preparing as much as she could for this, the next step in the game.

Book 6 of the Shadow Accords: Shadow Found

Carth has begun to develop her network, and offers her protection to the women of Asador, but not all are pleased with what she has done. When an assassin kills someone close to her, Carth leaves the city in pursuit. What she finds reveals that her plans have been inadequate, and the game she thought she had been playing might have been another entirely. If she doesn't adapt, those she's vowed to protect will be in danger, and a greater threat will be unleashed.

Looking for another great read? Soldier Son, Book 1 of The Teralin Sword, out now.

As the second son of the general of the Denraen, Endric wants only to fight, not the commission his father demands of him. When a strange attack in the south leads to the loss of someone close to him, only Endric seems concerned about what happened.

All signs point to an attack on the city, and betrayal by someone deep within the Denraen, but his father no longer trusts his judgment. This forces Endric to make another impulsive decision, one that leads him far from the city on a journey where he discovers how little he knew, and how much more he has to understand. If he can prove himself in time, and with the help of his new allies, he might be able to stop a greater disaster.

ABOUT THE AUTHOR

DK Holmberg currently lives in rural Minnesota where the winter cold and the summer mosquitoes keep him inside and writing.

Word-of-mouth is crucial for any author to succeed and how books are discovered. If you enjoyed the book, please consider leaving a review at Amazon, even if it's only a line or two; it would make all the difference and would be very much appreciated.

Subscribe to my newsletter to be the first to hear about giveaways and new releases.

For more information:

www.dkholmberg.com

dkh@dkholmberg.com

Born of Fire

Broken of Fire

Light of Fire

Cycle of Fire

Others in the Cloud Warrior Series

Prelude to Fire

Chasing the Wind

Drowned by Water

Deceived by Water

Salvaged by Water

The Endless War

Journey of Fire and Night

Darkness Rising

Endless Night

Summoner's Bond

Seal of Light

The Lost Garden

Keeper of the Forest

The Desolate Bond

Keeper of Light

Manufactured by Amazon.ca
Bolton, ON